THE STAR AND THE SWORD

The Star and the Sword

by Pamela Melnikoff

illustrated by Hans Schwarz

THE JEWISH PUBLICATION SOCIETY
Philadelphia-Jerusalem

First Published by
Valletine, Mitchell & Co. Ltd.,
Gainsborough House, 11 Gainsborough Road, London E11 1RS

Text copyright © 1965 by Pamela Melnikoff
Cover art copyright © 1994 by Richard Martin

First paperback edition, 1994, by The Jewish Publication Society,
1930 Chestnut Street, Philadelphia, PA 19103-4599, U.S.A.

Library of Congress Cataloging-in-Publication Data

Melnikoff, Pamela.
The star and the sword / by Pamela Melnikoff; illustrated by Hans
Schwarz. — 1st pbk. ed.
     p. cm.
"Based on my play The ransomed menorah, which won the Golden
Pen Award in 1962"—Foreword.
Summary: When a massacre of Jews in twelfth-century England leaves
Elvira and Benedict orphaned, they set out to find an uncle they
hardly know and have many adventures on their journey, including
meeting Robin Hood.
ISBN 0-8276-0528-5
[1. Jews—Great Britain—Fiction. 2. Great Britain—History—
Medieval period, 1066 - 1485—Fiction. 3. Orphans—Fiction.]
I. Schwarz, Hans, ill. II. Melnikoff, Pamela. Ransomed menorah.
III, Title.
PZ7.M5163St   1994
[Fic]—dc20
                                                              94-5813
                                                              CIP
                                                              AC

10   9   8   7   6   5   4   3

CONTENTS

FOR MY PARENTS

FOREWORD

This book is based on my play *The Ransomed Menorah*, which won the Golden Pen Award in 1962, a play-writing contest organised annually by the Jewish Education Committee of New York. The play was presented by the Jewish Theatre for Children at the Joan of Arc Playhouse, New York.

In re-writing *The Ransomed Menorah* as a novel, I have not kept closely to the text of the play, but have expanded it and included several incidents which could not be presented on the stage.

I ought to mention, by the way, that – though the historical background of the story is accurate – all the other incidents and characters (including Benedict and Elvira) are entirely fictitious.

ONE soft summer evening in the year 1192, two Crusader knights sat playing chess in a tent pitched on the edge of the small town of Maxenburg, in Germany.

It was peaceful in the tent; firelight flickered on the silver wine-goblets and on the tiny jewelled chessmen, and the knights sat in a pleasant silence broken only by an occasional cry of 'Check!' or '*J'adoube!*' But soon they became aware of noise outside the tent, of shouts and the clash of steel and the sound of running feet, and the knights frowned because it was growing more and more difficult for them to concentrate on their game.

And so at last one of the knights – the one whose tent it was – sent his squire to find out what all the clamour was about.

Very soon the boy came running back, looking excited.

'It's the Jews, sir', he announced. 'Our men have killed some Jews. Baron Vauxley tried to take something out of a synagogue . . . some silver bells, I think,

9

and one of the Jews tried to stop him. So we killed him and his friends, and we burned the synagogue ...'

His master frowned.

'This makes us look like hooligans,' he said. 'We must never forget that we are soldiers of Christ, fighting a holy war ...'

'But these Jews are friends of the Devil – don't forget that either, Ned,' interrupted his friend, and he took a noisy gulp of wine and wiped his mouth with his embroidered sleeve. 'Besides, these particular Jews deserve all they got. They spoiled our game of chess, didn't they?'

The other knight smiled.

'Yes, I hadn't thought of that. All the same, I think I'll ride into the town and see what my men are doing. If you don't mind being left alone, Will.'

'I shall be happy as long as your wine lasts,' replied Will, and he filled his goblet again and put his feet up on the chess table, where his boots left muddy streaks on the amber-inlaid wood.

So the knight named Ned called for his horse, and then rode into the heart of the small town of Maxenburg, whose angular wooden houses and twisting streets looked dim and ghostly in the moonlight.

Most of the citizens were indoors, scared by the recent clamour. King Richard the Lionheart's soldiers, riding through Germany on their way home from the Crusades, were not the most considerate of guests. But here and there a torch blazed among the shadows and a small knot of English soldiers gathered, some pushing each other and brawling, some singing drunken songs, and one or two showing off silver goblets and candlesticks taken from the plundered synagogue.

Soon the knight found himself riding along a silent street which he knew must be the Jewry because of its large stone houses, now fearfully shuttered. The cobbles made a hollow clang under his horse's hoofs. From the end of the street came a sinister glow; the ruins of the synagogue were still smouldering, every so often shooting little showers of sparks into the black, velvety sky.

The knight pulled up outside the dark hulk of the building, and dismounted. There was nothing to bar his way; the heavy iron-studded door of the synagogue had been wrenched off its hinges, and there were great gaps in the walls, and the roof was open to the luminous stars.

Leaving his horse stamping on the cobbles and shaking its jewelled bridle, the knight went into the synagogue, stepping first over heaps of smouldering rubble and then over the sprawling bodies of four or five Jews who had died while trying to defend the Holy Ark.

That they had failed was obvious, for the doors of the Ark were shattered, its velvet curtain ripped in pieces, and the scrolls had been dragged out and burned. Long tattered coils of scorched parchment still lay crackling on the ruined floor. But the silver pointers and crowns and tinkling bells that had adorned them, and the silver goblets and candlesticks that had been the pride of the small synagogue . . . all these were gone.

'Looted,' thought the knight. 'I wish my men would not stoop to looting, but how can I stop them?'

And then, as he was about to leave the synagogue, his iron-shod foot caught in the wreckage and clinked against something that rang with a metallic sound.

The knight knelt and pushed aside the rubble, and the moon and the stars and the glowing embers illuminated something that shone more brightly than all of them together.

It was a great golden candelabrum. But it was unlike any candelabrum the knight had ever seen before, for it had eight branches, and another jutting out in front like the prow of a ship, and soaring above it was a six-pointed star, like the star which all Jews wore to proclaim that they were inferior to good Christian men. And there were jewels around the base of the candelabrum, and on the tips of its branches, and the star glittered, the knight thought, like the Star of Bethlehem.

He lifted the candelabrum in his hands, and it was very heavy. 'The gem of their collection,' he thought, 'and they hid it here so that they could find it again.'

Well, *he* had found it first. The knight ran his fingers along the intricate moulding on the candelabrum, and wondered what to do with it. He longed to keep it, but he had never looted in his life. And yet, if he left it where it was, some of his men would certainly find it, and perhaps wrench out the jewels and melt down the gold and divide the spoil among themselves.

The knight shuddered at the thought. 'Sooner than let that happen,' he said to himself, '*I* had better take it. At least *I* can appreciate works of art, which is more than can be said for my men.'

And making these lame excuses to himself the knight carried the golden candelabrum out of the ruined synagogue and into the deserted street. His horse was still stamping on the cobbles and tossing its jewelled bridle. The saddle-bag was large and quite empty. Carefully the knight lowered the candelabrum into the bag, and it slid down into the leathery darkness and was lost from sight.

The knight heaved a little sigh of relief. Then he swung himself into the saddle, gave his horse's flank a pat, and cantered away into the darkness.

CHAPTER 1

The Strawberry Picnic

IF Benedict and Elvira had not decided to go straw-berry-picking in the woods near Lymford, one June morning in the year 1193, this story would never have been written.

Benedict was nearly thirteen, and Elvira was ten, and they lived with their parents and their six-year-old brother Richard in a stone house in the Jewry at Lymford, which was a small town set in the hollow of the hills, a few miles south of the great city of York.

They were Jewish children and their outings were few and far between. Jewish parents liked their sons and daughters to stay at home and study. But on this particular June morning the sky was a piercing blue over the turrets and thatched roof-tops of Lymford and over the green, distant hills, and the sun made the dew sparkle on every leaf in Father's herb garden. The fishpond gleamed like polished silver, while the warm air was full of the scent of mint and roses and lavender and gillyflowers. And mother decided that the wild strawberries must be ripe by now in the woods just outside Lymford. Father was very fond of strawberry tarts.

'So you may forget your lessons, just for one day. That is, of course, if Father agrees,' she told the children. 'Elvira has been looking a little pale just lately; the fresh air will do her good. Tell Father I said so.' And Benedict looked at Elvira, whose cheeks were as rosy as apples, and smiled mischievously. Mother smiled too, but the smile was in her eyes.

She was sitting in the solar, the room where the family spent their leisure hours, embroidering a new cloak for Elvira, and the rich cloth spilled in a scarlet cascade over her own deep blue kirtle, and the sunlight, streaming through the new glass window (glass was very rare and expensive, and Father was very proud of this splendid addition to his household treasures) sparkled on her snow-white coif with its fine gold veil. The needle flashed in her long white fingers, and Elvira looked on enviously.

'Never mind,' laughed Mother. 'Your sewing will improve. At least, let us hope it will. You're almost old enough to be married, and we can't have your poor husband going about in rags.'

Elvira's mouth drooped, and Benedict looked at her and winked. Mother and Father never tired of reminding their daughter that *other* girls were married by the time they were eleven or twelve, and that *other* girls could cook and sew. Most of Elvira's cooking found its way into the compost heap, and none of the garments she stitched could ever be worn.

'Don't look so worried, my poppet,' said Mother, and she patted Elvira's hand. 'Take the big basket from the kitchen, and ask Elfrida to give you some dinner, and see that you wear your oldest clothes. We can't have you spoiling that pretty dress with grass and mud, Elvira. And don't forget to ask Father's permission first.'

'We will, Madam,' said Benedict politely, and he kissed Mother's hand, and Elvira said 'Yes, Madam,' and curtsied. Then the children walked slowly out of the room, closing the door very gently behind them. But once they were outside they forgot their dignity and hurtled along the stone-walled corridor, whooping and laughing in their joy at having a whole day's holiday.

They slowed down as they approached the heavy wooden door that led to Father's surgery. Benedict knocked politely, then gently and gingerly pushed the door open. The children never knew what they might see when they put their heads round that door, and they had once been beaten for giggling at an unhappy patient who was pressing a live, wriggling toad against his face as a cure for warts.

Today, however, there were no toads, only Alaric the mercer, having his aching head anointed with a mixture of green rue, mustard seed and egg white. Elias, Father's apprentice, stood in a corner of the surgery, pounding up thyme and marjoram with a pestle and mortar, and the scent of the bruised leaves filled the room. Father looked up from his patient and saw Elvira sniffing the perfumed air appreciatively.

'Well?' he boomed in his deep voice, and though his face was stern his eyes twinkled under their shaggy brows. Father, the children often thought, was the finest-looking man in Lymford. He was a tall, stately figure in his moss-green, fur-trimmed robe; his beard was black and curling, and his hair curled, too, under his yellow cap. Beside him Alaric the mercer, whose headache he was trying to cure, looked like a little, meek grey donkey.

Benedict explained – a little nervously – about the outing, and Father drew his brows sharply together.

'A good excuse for getting away from your lessons,

eh?' he said. 'When *I* was your age I studied from morning till night, and *I* was beaten for slacking. Things were very different when *I* was young.'

Benedict, who had already received more beatings than he could remember, said nothing. But Elvira looked up at Father appealingly.

'Mother thought you might like some strawberry tarts, sir,' she said, and Father roared with laughter.

'So you appeal to my gluttony, do you, you cunning little wretch?' he said. 'Well, you may go *this* time, but on no account are you to take that young rogue with you, do you hear? I'll teach him a lesson – if it's the last thing I do!'

The 'young rogue' was Richard, who had disgraced himself that morning by taking one of Father's rare manuscripts into the garden and dropping it in the fish-pond. He had been soundly beaten and sent to Father's study to learn six psalms by heart before supper time. Benedict and Elvira felt sorry for him; to miss the strawberry picnic was a dreadful punishment. But all they said was 'Yes, sir. Thank you, sir.'

'And you might as well look into my study,' added Father, 'and make sure the rascal is learning his lessons. He might be meddling with another manuscript or playing at soldiers with my chessmen . . . I wouldn't put anything past him.'

So after they had changed into their oldest clothes and shoes, and gone to the kitchen to collect a huge plaited straw basket, and asked Elfrida, the servant, to give them a picnic dinner, they called in at Father's study to see what Richard was doing.

Now, the outside of the house was dark, heavy stone, but whenever the children entered Father's study they felt as though they were walking into another world. It was all crimson and gold, an Eastern-looking room with red velvet cushions and gold-embroidered hangings, and it was crammed with treasures . . . a gold spice-box, and silver goblets, and a set of gold and ivory chessmen, and hundreds of rare manuscripts. And in the middle of the room, on a mother-of-pearl table, stood the greatest treasure of all . . . a huge candelabrum, called a Menorah, that glittered like the sun.

Richard lifted a dirty, tear-stained face from his book as his brother and sister peered round the door.

'W-why are you dressed like that?' he asked, his swollen eyes opening wide in astonishment.

'We're going strawberry-picking,' explained Benedict gently, and Richard's face crumpled again.

'It's not fair,' he sobbed. 'To choose *today,* just when I can't go!'

'We didn't *choose* to go today; Mother suggested it,' said Benedict, and Elvira added soothingly, 'Never mind, poppet, we'll bring back some lovely strawberries specially for you.' But Richard refused to be comforted, and he threw his book on the floor and howled.

'He'll get over it,' Benedict murmured to Elvira as they ran down the narrow flight of steps that led to the street below. 'By the time we come back he'll be all smiles.' But as he spoke, Richard pressed his face against the study window, made a hideous face at them, and then withdrew.

'He really *is* a naughty boy,' said Elvira with a worried little frown. 'I don't know what's going to happen to him if he goes on like this.' But as she spoke she became aware of the sunshine and the deep blue sky and the soft summer air, and at once she felt happy again.

The children skipped gaily down the street, waving to the Jewish women who sat carding wool or spinning at their doors, and then they left the Jewry behind and turned towards the town square. It was market day, and the booths were all doing a brisk trade; stall-holders were crying their wares, townspeople and monks and soldiers from Lymford Castle jostling each other in the narrow streets, pigs waddling across the cobbles and nosing in the gutters for stray titbits, and above the noise and gaiety and confusion rose the merry clamour of church bells.

Benedict and Elvira, who were hardly ever allowed to visit the market, were entranced by the scene, and Elvira felt tempted to stop at the haberdasher's booth to buy a scarlet ribbon that exactly matched her new cloak. But Benedict reminded her that they had no time to linger, took her by the hand and pulled her firmly past the booths, past the gallows (which were empty, much to Elvira's relief; the thought of people being hanged made her feel quite sick), and past the stocks, where Egbert the fishmonger sat doing penance for selling stinking fish, his own unappetising wares heaped at his feet.

'Phew!' muttered Benedict, and he and Elvira held their noses and ran past the stalls so quickly that they almost collided with a tall man, richly dressed in scarlet and sables, who was standing at the corner of the street deep in conversation with a white-robed friar and two men-at-arms. The nobleman turned and scowled at them, and the children were shocked by the cruelty on his dark face.

'Do you know who that was?' murmured Benedict, as he and Elvira hurried towards the West gate.

'No. But he looks horrid.'

'That was Henry de Poulny.'

'The Governor of Lymford?' And Elvira stopped dead, shocked by what Benedict had told her.

'Yes. Father says he hates the Jews.'

'He looks as though he hates everybody.'

'Especially the Jews. He owes us money. He owes about a thousand pieces of gold to Uncle Hugo.'

'So much?' And Elvira, astonished, nearly dropped her end of the basket.

'Yes. Father says he's a dangerous man. He'll stop at nothing to wipe out his debts, Father says.'

'H-how?' quavered Elvira, and Benedict saw that he had said too much.

'Oh, I don't know,' he replied. 'He'll just make himself unpleasant, I suppose.'

By this time the children had reached the city gate. The watchman smiled in a friendly way as he let them through, and Elvira's spirits rose again. And when she saw the green, rolling hills, and the dark streak of woodland on the horizon, and the limestone crags far beyond, with sheep grazing on the slopes and golden eagles circling in the deep blue overhead, she felt like dancing.

'We'll take this path; it leads to the woods,' said Benedict, and he and Elvira set off through the meadows, feeling as though this were the beginning of some tremendous adventure.

It was. But the children were not to guess, at that moment, that the happenings of the next few hours would alter their lives for ever.

CHAPTER 2

Clifford's Tower

'IT'S getting warm, isn't it?' said Elvira, and she mopped her streaming forehead with her apron. 'Let's sit down and rest for a few minutes.'

The path, which had led at first through flat green fields, was now winding steeply up the hillside, and the strawberry woods on the other side seemed a long way off.

'We'll rest when we get to the top; it's not very far,' said Benedict cheerfully, and Elvira sighed to herself and plodded on after him.

But she had her reward when they at last reached a grassy plateau and Benedict suggested that they sit down for a while to eat some fruit and enjoy the view.

In fact, she did not know which she liked better, the fat, rosy cherries, picked that morning in their own garden, or the sight of the countryside spread out beneath them like a vast map. From the top of their hill the fields, divided into strips by turf hedges, looked like a striped cloak; the serfs in the meadows below were as small as beetles; the occasional village was visible only as a church tower and a wisp of smoke

20

emerging from a clump of trees, and the music of the church bells sounded very faint and far away.

'Isn't there a lot of forest?' said Elvira, in some surprise, and Benedict nibbled at another cherry, and nodded.

'Most of it belongs to the king,' he explained. 'He hunts there.'

'What does he hunt?'

'Oh, I don't know. Wolves, I suppose, and deer, and boars, and bison. Wild animals.'

'D-do you think w-*we* might meet any?'

Benedict laughed. 'Don't worry,' he said. '*We're* only going into the strawberry wood, and there aren't any wild beasts there. Nothing very exciting is going to happen to *us.*'

'No, I don't suppose we'll ever have any adventures,' agreed Elvira, suddenly feeling a little wistful. 'I'll get married when I'm twelve, like Rebecca, and I'll never go strawberry-picking or play games any more. And you'll be a physician like Father, and you'll sit in a dull old surgery all day curing people's warts and headaches. And we'll never go anywhere. I don't suppose we'll ever see London in the whole of our lives.'

'Cheer up!' replied Benedict, and he patted her hand. 'Adventures aren't always much fun. Specially when you happen to be Jewish. Look, do you see that grey tower on the horizon, the one near that big cluster of spires?'

Elvira followed his pointing finger, and nodded.

'Those are the spires of York, and that is Clifford's Tower,' said Benedict slowly, and there was no laughter in his voice now.

'Clifford's Tower? Where the Jews of York hid? Where they . . .?'

Elvira knew all about the Jews of York, although

she had been only seven when it had happened. She knew how they had crowded into Clifford's Tower to escape from the angry mob, and how they had all died there. Now, as she remembered, a chill seemed to come into the sunlit morning.

'It happened a long time ago,' she thought. 'It couldn't happen in Lymford. Not to us.'

Benedict, seeing how pale she looked, quickly changed the subject.

'I think we must move on, or there'll be no time to pick any strawberries, and Father won't get his strawberry tarts, and he'll beat us for wasting *a whole day*.'

Benedict said this in a deep booming voice so like Father's that Elvira giggled and scrambled to her feet.

Now the path led downhill, and the children soon found themselves in the meadows, gazing up at a strange contraption with four great arms, all made of wooden slats, which carved slow circles in the flower-scented air.

'It's one of those new-fangled windmills,' explained Benedict, and he made a scornful face. 'Father says they'll never catch on.'

Soon the children came to the wood where the wild strawberries grew. It seemed very dim and cool after the warmth and brightness of the meadows; the trees laced their green branches overhead, and the glades were full of wild roses and silvery clumps of daisies. And then they found the strawberries, fat red berries half-hidden in leaves, and they began to fill the basket and their mouths alternately.

The rest of the day passed quickly. At noon the children ate the picnic dinner Elfrida had packed for them – chicken pasty and hard-boiled eggs and cherry tart – and drank home-made elderberry wine out of a goatskin flagon. After that, Benedict felt sleepy, so he stretched out on the grass and closed his eyes blissfully, while Elvira made daisy-chains and twined them round his head.

'Hasn't it been a wonderful day?' she sighed, as he woke, rubbed his eyes, and began to pick the wilting daisy-heads out of his thick brown hair. 'I feel so sorry for Richard; *he* would have enjoyed it. Especially the picnic dinner.'

'There'll be more outings,' replied Benedict with a big-brother smile. 'He's young yet.'

'And I suppose this *will* be a lesson to him,' added Elvira, as she and Benedict finished heaping the basket high with ripe strawberries.

The sun was already low in the sky when they left the wood and began to climb the path up the hillside, carrying the laden basket between them. A rich gold light seemed to fill the whole world, and they heard a ploughman singing as he drove his oxen homewards, and a shepherd-boy piping on a reed flute as he gathered his lambs together.

'*Hasn't* it been a beautiful day?' said Elvira again, with a little sigh. 'I'll remember it as long as I live. I wonder how long it will be before we have another outing.'

Because the children were so reluctant to return home, it seemed no time at all before the earthen ramparts of Lymford loomed up against the sunset sky.

'We'd better go in by the South gate; it's more direct, and we're late already,' said Benedict. The South gate led straight to the Jewry, by-passing the town square. Elvira was disappointed – she had looked forward to another glimpse of the market – but to arrive home late for supper meant a beating from Father. So she followed Benedict obediently to the South gate.

'Hallo, where's the watchman?' exclaimed Benedict

in surprise. Elvira followed his glance and saw that the watch-tower was empty, though the gate was still open and curfew had not yet sounded.

'Perhaps he had a headache,' she suggested wisely.

'He'll get into trouble if the Governor finds out,' said Benedict. 'Still, it's no business of ours. Come along.'

He stooped to pick up his end of the basket. Then, suddenly, he gripped Elvira's arm.

'Look . . . through there . . . Through the arch . . . Can you see anything?' he whispered.

Elvira looked. She could see nothing . . . only a red glow that might have been the setting sun.

'But the sun doesn't *set* in that direction,' cried Benedict, as though he guessed her thoughts.

'Then what is it?'

A cloud of dark smoke suddenly billowed high above the stone archway, and Elvira was answered.

CHAPTER 3

De Poulny Pays his Debts

NOW, don't get worried,' said Benedict urgently, trying to sound calm, although he had turned pale. 'It's a house on fire, that's all ...'

'I-it might be ours.'

'And it might not. You *are* a worrier, aren't you? Let's go and find out. It's probably just an accident. Somebody's been careless.'

But it was not an accident. Benedict knew it in his heart, even before he and Elvira turned into the Jewry and saw the great stone houses spurting smoke and fire from their gaping windows. The heavy doors had been smashed or torn from their hinges, and the children could hear the sound of shouting and laughter and drunken singing coming from the depths of those grave, sedate houses.

'W-what's happened?' quavered Elvira.

'Ssssh!' Benedict gripped her arm and pulled her into one of the gaping doorways. Not a moment too soon, for one of the revellers suddenly lurched out of the doorway across the street. It was Tom the chandler, a lanky mild-looking man who had once come to Father's surgery to be cured of the ague. But he did not look mild now; he was laughing uproariously, and his tunic was stained with wine. One hand swung a chopper, and in the other hand he clutched a huge golden candelabrum.

'That's ours! He's stealing our Menorah!' hissed Elvira, so aghast that she forgot to lower her voice.

'Sssssh!'

'But he's stealing it . . .'

Benedict clapped his hand over Elvira's mouth and pulled her further into the doorway, and the children watched as Tom the chandler polished the Menorah on his dirty tunic, held it up all glittering against the glowing sky, and then staggered into the doorway of the adjoining house.

'It's wicked to steal . . .' began Elvira furiously, but her words were suddenly drowned by a burst of drunken laughter from the dark hall behind her. Then came the clatter of boots on the paving-stones, and Benedict grabbed Elvira by the hand and ran down the street, pulling her desperately after him.

Elvira had never run so fast in her life. Her shoes tore on the sharp cobbles; her heart thumped so that she could scarcely breathe; the dark smoke swirled about her and made her cough – and it was not till she and Benedict had reached the end of the street that she realised that they had dropped their basket, and that the precious strawberries were rolling like discarded rubies in the gutter.

'W-where are we going?'

'The market-place,' gasped Benedict. 'There are people there. We'll be safe.'

But when the children actually reached the market-place, with its gay little booths and stalls, Benedict realised that he had been wrong. Horribly wrong.

Almost all the townsfolk seemed to be massed in the

square, under the darkening sky, streaked now with the last of its crimson and gold. Some of them held blazing torches; some brandished daggers and staves and axes; some were gnawing chunks of bread and meat or quaffing tankards of wine; some were laughing or singing or shouting. And then someone with a loud voice began to yell 'Kill them; kill the Jews!' and other voices took up the cry till the roofs and rafters and darkening Heavens seemed to ring with it.

And then the children saw that all the Jews of Lymford were huddled in a little knot in the centre of the square, hemmed in on all sides by the yelling townsfolk. Their own family stood in the forefront – Father with his arms firmly folded; Mother with her golden veil glimmering in the twilight, and Richard, frightened and subdued, clutching at her hand. Facing the group of Jews was a white-robed friar holding aloft a crucifix, and by his side stood a tall man in scarlet and sables, with a mighty sword in his hand, and when he turned his head for an instant, the children recognised his dark, cruel face.

'It's Henry de Poulny,' thought Benedict. 'Henry de Poulny . . . about to wipe out his debts for ever.'

All at once the friar shouted 'Who will help me rid the world of the enemies of Christ?', and the crowd surged forward, axes and clubs raised, shouting in triumph.

'Come away,' cried Benedict, and he seized Elvira's hand again and pulled her out of the horrible market-place, and the two children ran blindly till they found themselves in the quiet darkness of a side street. There they sank down in a doorway, their legs trembling, too dazed with shock even to realise the true meaning of what they had seen.

'I'm cold,' whimpered Elvira, and Benedict wrapped

his cloak round her shoulders.

'Did you see their faces?' he whispered. 'They looked different. Sort of . . . sort of mad. Not like themselves at all.'

Suddenly a torch flared up out of the shadows, and a pair of heavy shoes came thumping over the cobbles. The children shrank back into the doorway, but the torchlight soon picked them out, and in its glow they saw the anxious face of Alaric the mercer.

'Ah, I thought it was you,' he said. 'I saw you creep out of the market-place. Don't be scared; I won't hurt you.'

'W-what's happening? W-what started it all?' demanded Benedict, dismayed to find that his voice was trembling.

'Money,' replied Alaric. 'They that owed money to the Jews, *they* started it. Baron de Poulny, *he* was the first. He owed a lot of money to the Jews. Down in the market-place they're burning the deeds now. The king will be angry when he comes home.'

'D-deeds?'

'The deeds that prove they owe money to the Jews. They've dragged them out of the Jews' houses, and they're burning them. Baron de Poulny – *he* started it. Nothing to do with me. *I* don't owe money to no-one.'

A sudden burst of laughter came from the end of the street, and Alaric grabbed at Elvira's hand. 'Come to my house,' he muttered. 'Quick. You'll be safe there. Don't worry, I won't hurt you. I wouldn't do nothing like that.'

Trembling, the children huddled close behind Alaric, starting each time a shadow moved or a wooden shutter creaked in the evening breeze. It seemed hours (though it was only minutes) before they came to a thatched cottage near the East gate.

'You'd best go down into the cellar,' said Alaric.

'You'll be safe there, and you can slip away before dawn. I'll bring you something to eat.'

He opened a heavy wooden door, and by the smouldering light of his torch the children saw a flight of damp stone steps leading into what looked like a dark pit.

Shuddering with fear and cold, the children tumbled into the cellar. Then Alaric slammed the door after them, and they heard his shoes clumping away into the darkness.

Left alone, Benedict and Elvira clung together in a kind of numb horror. It was damp and cold in the cellar, and the air was full of the heavy dank smell of dyed woollen cloth. They were aware of the invisible bales stacked high all around them. None of the mob would ever think of searching for them there.

How strange it was, thought Benedict with a wry little smile. Only that morning Father had been treating Alaric's headache, and Alaric had looked like a little grey donkey beside the tall, handsome physician. And now Father was probably dead, and Alaric was a giant, a champion to keep the children from harm.

'D-do you think they escaped?' murmured Elvira at last.

'Who?'

'F-father and Mother and Richard? And the others?'

'Perhaps,' said Benedict, trying to sound cheerful.

'How will we know?'

'Alaric will find out for us.'

'He's a nice man. It's funny . . . we never really knew him, did we?'

'We never really knew any of them,' replied Benedict, remembering the blazing eyes and the daggers and the shouting in the market-square.

After a while Alaric returned, bringing bread and cheese and two mugs of mulled wine. The children drank the hot wine gratefully, and munched the bread and cheese, suddenly aware that they were hungry. The strawberry picnic, the chicken pasty and cherry tart in the rose-spattered glade, seemed a thousand years ago.

Slowly the night wore on. It was, Benedict thought, the longest night of their lives. 'What shall we do if they're all dead?' he asked himself. 'What will become of us?'

And then, out of the blurring images of his early childhood, came a memory. Horses being saddled; food and fine gifts and rich attire being crammed into the saddlebags; Father and Mother and Uncle Hugo setting out on the long journey to Oxford. And then their return, full of stories of the family wedding they had attended and the hospitality they had received from Mother's brother, who was one of the leaders of Oxford's Jewry.

'We'll go to Oxford,' announced Benedict suddenly. 'To Uncle Isaac. *He'll* give us a home. I know he will.'

'H-how will we get there?' quavered Elvira.

'We'll walk. How else?'

It was almost dawn when Alaric came back. He opened the cellar door, and the children smelled the sweet, cool air and glimpsed a patch of amethyst sky.

'It's almost the end of curfew time,' he whispered. 'The watchmen are off to open the gates – and if you're going to slip away it had better be now. Have you anywhere to go?'

'Oxford,' replied Benedict, glad to have an answer. 'Our uncle lives there.'

Alaric nodded.

'You'd better take this,' he added, handing them

a cloth-wrapped bundle on the end of a stick. 'It's some bread and cheese, and a flask of ale. And here's a silver penny for you. I reckon you'll need it.'

Benedict thanked the mercer, but it was Elvira who chimed in with the question he had been afraid to ask.

'Father and Mother? Is there any news?'

'I've been all over the town, and I've spoken to everyone,' replied Alaric sadly. 'There's not a Jew left alive in the whole of Lymford. There's not a thing of value left in any of their houses; it's all been took. *I* had nothing to do with it, I promise you.'

The sun was rising as the children passed through the East gate and out into the world. It was a beautiful morning, as beautiful as the morning before had been, which had begun so happily. The sky was a blue haze over the pointed roofs and the distant hills; dew sparkled in the gardens; the birds were singing their early morning song, and church bells were beginning to chime out over the countryside. But the Jews of Lymford, and the safe, happy life the children had always known, were vanished as though they had never been.

CHAPTER 4

The Outlaws

ARE we far from Oxford?' whimpered Elvira.

There was a blister on her heel, and she longed to rest for a while, but Benedict had insisted that they put as many miles as they could between themselves and Lymford.

'Far enough,' replied Benedict.

'When will we get there?'

'In a few days.'

'A few *days*?' And Elvira, too shocked to walk any further, flopped down on the grass, glad of an excuse to rest her aching legs.

'Of course. Did you think we would be there tonight?' said Benedict, smiling in spite of himself.

'But we can't go on walking for *days*.'

'We've no choice.'

'What will we eat?'

'We can beg.'

Elvira looked up at her brother in horror. She had seen beggars, hundreds of them, during the happy times in Lymford. They looked like living bundles of rags, and sometimes they were deformed or covered with sores, and rich people fed them. She herself had often carried leftover loaves and dishes of cold chicken and fish from the Sabbath and Festival tables to distribute among the beggars who gathered at Father's door, and they had always blessed her and prayed that she might never know poverty. And now *she* would be a beggar like them. Elvira had been too stunned to cry when she learned that her parents and Richard were dead, but now her eyes filled with tears.

Benedict patted her hand kindly.

'Don't worry,' he said. 'We won't starve. People will give us food. You'll see.'

'But...'

'Anyway, we've still got some bread and cheese left. And a silver penny to buy more.'

'Let's have some bread now,' pleaded Elvira, wiping away her tears with a grimy fist. 'I'm starving. We haven't eaten for years and years.'

So Benedict carefully cut two small slices from the remains of the loaf Alaric had given him and the children tried to make them last by eating them very slowly.

'We'll have a drink of water at the next brook,' said Benedict, as he diligently sucked the crumbs from his fingers. Then he looked at Elvira, and smiled mischievously.

'I was just thinking,' he said, 'that no one would ever recognise us as the well-bred children of Simon the Physician. If Father could see us now, he would thrash us.'

Elvira looked at him, hot and grubby in his oldest tunic, and then glanced down at her own grass-stained skirt. Their clothes bore the marks of the meadows and of Alaric's dusty cellar. Both she and Benedict were beginning to grow tanned by the sun and the wind. And her hair, her long, black hair which

Mother had always combed so carefully, so that it hung over her shoulders like a silk cape, was as snarled as the hair of a beggar-woman.

'We *do* look a mess,' she agreed sadly. 'I've never been so dirty in my whole life.'

'It's just as well,' replied Benedict. 'At least no one will take us for Jews now.'

And both children grew silent, remembering what had happened to those other Jews in the market square, and they shivered, in spite of the noon-day sun.

They had been walking, with only a short pause for food, since their flight from Lymford. And now the city of death was far behind, and all around them lay the tranquil green countryside. Meadows and farms and wheat-fields and orchards heavy with blossom; wisps of blue-grey smoke floating from hidden roofs into the deeper blue of the sky; every so often the stone splendour of a manor; here and there a team of oxen drawing a wooden plough, a group of serfs weeding or haymaking or a boy gathering flax, and, all along the horizon, the dark green ramparts of the waiting forest.

No one as much as glanced at Benedict and Elvira, and they realised how lucky they were to have been wearing their strawberry-picnicking clothes at the time of the massacre. In their everyday clothes of velvet and fine Eastern-style embroidery they would at once have been recognised as Jews. But now they could pass quite easily as Saxon peasants. Shabby, dirty children were a common enough sight in the Saxon countryside.

'We shall have to think of a story,' Benedict went on. 'Something to tell people when they ask why we're walking to Oxford.'

'Why not tell them the truth?' replied Elvira meekly.

'The *truth*? and risk being killed? It *could* happen again; don't forget that.'

'B-but there must be *some* nice Christians,' protested Elvira. 'After all, l-look at Alaric.'

'We can't take the risk,' said Benedict. 'People mustn't know we're Jews. We could say . . . wait – I'll think of something.'

'Couldn't we say we were strolling players?' said Elvira hopefully. 'Or troubadours?'

'We don't look the least bit like strolling players,' replied Benedict patiently. 'And troubadours carry harps, and sing ballads.'

'Well then, *you* suggest something,' said Elvira, a little piqued.

Benedict shut his eyes, thought hard, and then opened them in triumph.

'Apprentices,' he cried. 'We'll be apprentices, running away from a cruel master. Egbert the Fishmonger used to beat his apprentices, remember? And they were always running away.'

'That's a wonderful idea,' said Elvira, forgetting to be annoyed with Benedict. 'A nasty cruel master, who beat us.'

'And locked us in the cellar, and fed us on dry crusts. He can be a shoemaker. Gurth the shoemaker. We'll tell people he used to beat us with his little hammer. We'll say we're going to friends in Oxford, who can give us honest employment. We'd better change our names too; ours are so Jewish. I'll be John, I think, and you can be Alice.'

The children were soon able to put their story to the test. Late in the afternoon, after tramping for what seemed like miles through barren scrub-land, they came to a hut in a rough clearing, a tumble-down hut of mud and wattles, thatched with reeds. A smoky peat fire belched and spluttered on a heap of stones outside the hut; an earthenware cauldron squatted among the flames, and an unkempt, barefoot woman, dressed in dirty sackcloth, knelt in front of it, stirring something that smelt delicious. Quite forgetting their manners, the children stood and stared.

'Beans,' said the woman, as though she read their thoughts. 'It's bean broth. Are you hungry?'

Speechless, the children nodded.

'Well, you've come at a good time; we're just about to have supper,' said the woman, and she chuckled, showing a few blackened stumps of teeth. 'My husband will soon be back from the woods. You'd best come inside, and then we'll eat.' She lifted the pot in her two leathery hands, and gestured for the children to follow her.

The inside of the hut was dark and cold; it seemed a place where spring and summer never penetrated. Walls and floor of bare, trodden earth, two wooden benches, a heap of mouldering straw in one corner, and a few wooden bowls and spoons, and that was all.

'So this is poverty,' thought Benedict sadly. 'We've lived sheltered lives till now, Elvira and I.'

A few minutes later their host arrived home. He was a swineherd, a huge bearded man in a rabbit-skin tunic, and his charges came waddling and grunting after him in noisy confusion. The children watched in dismay as the pigs followed their master into the hut and made themselves comfortable in one corner. When, soon afterwoods, the couple's three children came home, all laden with brushwood, the hut began to grow very cramped indeed.

But the bean broth tasted delicious to the hungry children – though they were not used to such simple fare – and their hosts were very kind. When Benedict told them about Gurth, the cruel shoemaker, they shook their heads in disapproval; when Elvira told them how she and Benedict had been fed on dry crusts, they tut-tutted sympathetically, and when Benedict described how he and Elvira had been thrashed with the shoemaker's little hammer, the swineherd clenched his fists so fiercely that even the pigs trembled.

'I know exactly what you have to put up with,' he thundered. 'I am a bondman to Lord William de Rougemont, and he has *me* beaten if my work doesn't please him. But *I* can't run away; I've a family to support. Ah, it's a sad thing when we English are poor and downtrodden and the Normans and the Jews have all the money.'

Elvira trembled, and looked down into her bowl of broth, and Benedict pressed her arm in warning.

'But perhaps *you* have Norman blood,' added the swineherd, looking at Elvira curiously. 'The little girl's hair is too dark to be pure Saxon.'

'My grandmother was French,' said Benedict quickly, glad to be given an opportunity to tell the truth (for grandmother Janetta *had* been French), and Elvira blushed. Both children felt relieved when their hostess announced that it was bed-time, and they were glad to lie down on a bundle of straw in a dark corner of the hut, away from inquisitive eyes.

Neither Benedict nor Elvira slept very much that night. They lay huddled together, listening to the snorts and grunts of the pigs and the snores of their human companions, and breathing the dank smell of earth and rotting straw, and it was like Alaric's cellar all over again.

'Suppose there is no refuge in Oxford?' thought Benedict. 'Suppose we find *them* murdered when we arrive? What will we do then? Will all our lives be spent like this?'

But he did not say a word to Elvira.

The children were glad to leave their hosts next morning, despite their kindness. After the smoky darkness of the hut, the dawn air smelt as sweet as roses. The swineherd and his wife filled their empty flask with ale before they left, and gave them a loaf of black bread. They would have given them a meat pie, too, but Benedict, remembering the Jewish laws about food and tearing his eyes reluctantly from its golden crust, explained that he and Elvira had a stomach complaint and were not allowed to eat meat.

'That's a pity,' said their hostess, 'with bread the price it is. If it wasn't for the pigs, we should starve.'

Benedict and Elvira were forced to refuse meat many times more during the next few days, and often went hungry as a result. Bread was scarce, and few people were willing to part with it. On the next night the children slept in the kitchen of a baronial hall, fed with left-overs by a kindly cook; the following night they spent in the shelter of a hedgerow, after supping on a slice of stale barley bread. And all the time they tramped steadily southwards, across meadows and vast moors and through marshes and scrub and great stretches of primeval forest.

The people they met believed their story about Gurth the shoemaker, and very soon the children almost came to believe it themselves. Sometimes it seemed that they could even remember their lives as apprentices, and Lymford and that last sunset in the market-square dwindled into a dream they had both had, long ago.

About a week after leaving Lymford the children found themselves passing through a forest named Sherwood, in Nottinghamshire. They were both limping now, and Elvira's shoes were worn almost to tatters. A farmer had given them a lift in his cart as far as the edge of the forest, but now they were alone again, and their exhausted legs could scarcely carry them.

'We *must* reach the next village before sunset,' said Benedict urgently, taking Elvira's arm with a jauntiness he did not feel. 'If we don't, we shall have to sleep in the forest, and . . .'

He did not finish the sentence, but Elvira knew what he meant. Everybody knew that there were wild beasts in the woods, who came out at night to hunt for food. Sometimes, in winter, they came as far as the towns and villages. There had been one long winter, with snow lying thick on the ground for weeks, when wolves had prowled and howled at the very gates of Lymford. And now there were no gates, no high and sturdy walls, to protect her and Benedict.

She looked at the heavily-massed trees that crowded in upon them like the columns of some ancient temple, and shuddered.

But although she and Benedict walked as fast as they could on their blistered feet, the first fiery glow of sunset found them still in the heart of Sherwood.

'We'll never make it,' muttered Benedict. 'We shall *have* to spend the night here. Perhaps I can make a fire with a bit of tinder-wood.'

It was at that moment that the children seemed to hear the distant, the far-distant cry of a horn floating mournfully through the darkening colonnades of the forest.

'The Shofar,' whispered Benedict, forgetting for a moment where he was. 'Listen, Elvira . . . it sounds like the Shofar . . .'

And he and Elvira held hands and listened to the horn, which sounded so like the ram's horn that calls the Jews to prayer during their most solemn festivals. And they began to remember slim white candles, and the chanting of the cantor, and the velvet-covered scrolls, and carp and roast chicken and honey-cakes and wine.

'Why did all this have to happen?' wept Elvira. 'Why couldn't life just go on, the way it always did?'

The horn sounded again, its echoes hanging plaintively in the purple air. Then a man stepped out of the shadow of the trees. He was tall, broadly-built, dressed in a green tunic and breeches and a plumed hat, and a horn dangled from a leather strap about his waist.

At first he did not see the children. Then his glance fell on them, and his eyes grew stern.

'What are you doing here?' he said sharply. 'Who sent you?'

'N-no one,' faltered Benedict. And he began to tell the story of Gurth the shoemaker, while Elvira, trembling, cowered behind him.

The man's grim expression softened, and he glanced down at the children's grimy clothes and worn-out shoes. Then he smiled and held out both his hands to them.

'You may stay here as long as you like, and accept our hospitality,' he said. 'No harm will come to you in Sherwood. You have my word for it. I am Robin Hood.'

CHAPTER 5

Strangers in Sherwood

A FEW days later, a stranger rode into Sherwood Forest.

He was a fat, middle-aged man with a pompous, pasty face and little bright eyes. His clothes were expensive . . . a bliaut, or tunic, of fine blue wool over a linen under-tunic; a rich crimson cloak fastened at the shoulder with a gold brooch, and stout leather boots. A heavy leather money-bag hung from his belt. And he rode his horse, which was a sleek, fat chestnut, with an air which seemed to say 'I am an important man, and don't let anyone forget it!'

He reined sharply as two men stepped out of the shadow of the trees. One was tall and lanky and dressed all in scarlet; the other, taller still and broadly-built, with a mop of carroty hair.

'You are Henry Shepherd, I believe,' said the scarlet-clad man with a polite little bow.

'I don't think I have the honour of your acquaintance,' replied the man on horseback coldly.

The red-haired man chuckled.

'You know us well enough, Master Shepherd,' he

said. 'I am Little John, and this gentleman is Will Scarlett, and we are followers of Robin Hood, who is Lord of this forest. We met once on the way to Nottingham Fair, and you very kindly gave us some money. Remember?'

Henry Shepherd scowled.

'You're a lot of thieves and vagabonds, that's what you are,' he snapped. 'I wish *I* were Sheriff of Nottingham; I would clean up this forest and hang you all, together with your precious Robin Hood. An honest man can't pass through Sherwood these days without fear of getting robbed.'

Both Outlaws hooted with laughter.

'Did you say an *honest* man, Master Shepherd?' said Little John. 'It all depends, of course, what one means by honest. Now *I* personally feel that a landlord who grows fat on the misery of his tenants is no more honest than a man who snatches purses. In fact, *we* are more honest, because we rob the rich to help the poor.'

'How dare you suggest that *I* rob my tenants!' snapped Henry Shepherd, his face dark with fury. 'At least *I'm* not a rogue who doesn't dare show his face in public, among decent men.'

'Now, don't let's quarrel,' replied Will Scarlett soothingly. 'Let's all be friends. We only want to ask you a small favour, Master Shepherd. Just a tiny little gift . . . say fifty pieces of gold . . . to help bring our Lord the King back from captivity in Austria.'

'I've already given my share of the tax to de Bourg, the official collector,' said Henry Shepherd loftily, 'and I won't give a penny more. I wouldn't, even if I could afford it. I've never thought very highly of your precious Richard the Lionheart. If it came to a choice of kings I would give my vote to Prince John.'

'Treachery!' cried Will Scarlett, in mock horror. 'Do you know that what you have said is high treason?'

'And will *you* dare accuse me?' sneered Henry Shepherd.

Little John stepped forward, seized the horse's bridle, and brandished a huge fist in Henry Shepherd's face.

'Enough of this idle chit-chat,' he growled. 'Will you give us fifty pieces of gold, sir, or shall we give you a bloody nose?'

Henry Shepherd cowered back, and his pasty face turned even yellower.

'Now, John, don't frighten the gentleman,' said Will Scarlett. 'I'm sure he's only too willing to help us.' And he began gently to unhook the money-bag from Henry Shepherd's belt.

'I'll have the law on you,' moaned the landlord feebly. 'Thieves and vagabonds, that's what you are!'

Little John, quite unperturbed by this threat, weighed the money-bag in his hand. Then he again seized the horse's bridle.

'I think this animal would be happier here with us,' he said. 'A harsh landlord is hardly likely to prove a kind master, is he?'

Henry Shepherd's face now began to take on a brick-red hue.

'D-do you mean,' he spluttered, 'that you intend to steal my horse as well?'

'We're only keeping it here for its own good,' explained Will Scarlett with a sweet smile. 'Horses benefit by a change of scenery, just like humans. You want your horse to benefit, don't you? Besides, *we* could do with another horse.'

'I-I-I'll have the law on you,' Henry Shepherd began, but here Little John seized him by the neck of his tunic, dragged him out of the saddle, and again raised his fist in a threatening gesture.

'If you dare say *one* word about us to anyone, Henry Shepherd,' he roared, 'I'll chop you into little pieces and eat you for my supper. Now begone, before I get angry!'

'H-how shall I get home?' whimpered the landlord.

'You can walk,' replied Little John. 'It'll do you good. You're much too fat. Just look at that belly of yours!' And he prodded Henry Shepherd's bulging paunch none too gently.

The Outlaws laughed as the angry landlord set off at a brisk pace, shaking his fist and swearing vengeance on Robin Hood and all his followers. But after he had gone, Will Scarlett's face grew serious.

'He's an important man in these parts, isn't he?' he said. 'I reckon he could be a dangerous enemy.'

'What, *that* fat idiot?' replied Little John scornfully, and he patted Henry Shepherd's horse, which was staring after its departing master in some surprise. 'Forget him. He wouldn't dare say a word about us, the coward.'

'He knows the Sheriff.'

'So do we. Don't worry, Will. We've heard the last of him, I promise you. But look, here comes my sweetheart, and she's prettier than ever today.'

These last words were addressed to Elvira, who had come dancing into the glade at that moment with her hands full of buttercups. She was followed by a stout man in a friar's habit, his jovial face beaming under a rosebud coronet.

Little John roared with laughter.

'So she's got you all dressed up like the Queen of the May, has she, Friar Tuck?' he guffawed. 'Don't let Alan-a-Dale see you, or he'll write a ballad in praise of your beauty.'

'Well, that would make a pleasant change,' replied Friar Tuck in his deep booming voice. 'But it's little Alice here who looks like the Queen of the May, not *me*.'

Elvira glanced up with a smile. She was used, by now, to being called Alice, and to having a dozen men in Lincoln green to tease her and dance attendance on her. She and Benedict had been in Sherwood for three days now, and they loved the life . . . the comradeship, sunlight or moonlight slanting through the green roof of the forest, feasting and singing round the great bonfire, and the feeling, at last, that they were safe among friends.

But the children knew that it could not last long – that they must soon move on towards Oxford. They were aware, too, that Robin Hood and his merry men might be less friendly if they knew that their young guests were Jewish, and they were always on guard, lest a slip of the tongue betray them.

Will Scarlett lifted Elvira and swung her high in the air.

'And where's your brother today, my poppet?' he said.

'He's with Robin, learning to shoot,' she replied.

'And he's doing well, too,' chuckled Friar Tuck. 'Knows one end of an arrow from the other already. Any day now he'll go out and bring us back a nice fat deer.'

'Much good it will do him,' snorted Little John. 'Unless he learns to eat good venison. And you too, little maid. I've never come across children before who didn't like meat. You'll never grow big and strong on bread and vegetables.'

'We both had the fever,' explained Elvira for the tenth time that week, 'and the physician told us never to eat meat again.'

'That's very strange,' beamed Friar Tuck. '*I* had the fever twenty years ago, and I've eaten twice as much as other men ever since.'

'Twice as much? *Three* times, *I* would have said,' declared Little John. 'But, while we're talking about a nice fat deer, I must tell you . . . Will and I have just taken fifty gold pieces off Henry Shepherd.'

'*And* a horse,' added Will Scarlett cheerfully.

'Good. Very good,' said Friar Tuck. 'We'll have *something,* at least, to give Sir Edward when he arrives here next week.'

Benedict and Elvira already knew that King Richard was a prisoner in Austria, that his captors had demanded a ransom of a hundred thousand pounds, and that the money was being raised in tax from the British people. (As always, the Jews had been forced to contribute twice as much as anyone else). Now, from Robin Hood and his Outlaws, they learned that Sir Edward de Bourg, a gallant knight who had fought under King Richard in the Crusades, was collecting ransom tax in the North of England. He was due to make his final call in Sherwood Forest, and to accept Robin Hood's hospitality for a few days, before galloping to London to deliver the ransom money to the Queen.

A few days after Henry Shepherd had made his second contribution to the royal ransom, two more strangers rode into Sherwood Forest.

It was Tom, the Outlaws' official look-out man, who saw them first. Flushed with excitement, he ran to break the news to Robin Hood, who was relaxing in a green glade, his merry men about him, while Alan-a-Dale sang a plaintive love song to the lute.

'It's two Jews,' he cried. 'Jew merchants, with heavy money-bags. They're on their way to Nottingham Fair, I'll be bound!'

'And straight into our welcoming arms,' chuckled Little John. 'Well, another little contribution to the king's ransom won't come amiss.'

None of the outlaws saw Benedict and Elvira grow pale and turn to look at each other. Nor did they see Benedict place a warning finger on his lips. They were all watching, instead, as Robin Hood rose to his feet, brushed the grass from his tunic, and slowly drew a gleaming dagger from his belt.

'We'll just *show* them our weapons,' he said with a smile. 'No violence, my friends. They don't need any. Jews always do as they are told.'

'Just fifty pieces of gold apiece,' added Will Scarlett.

'I don't see why they should pay more than Henry Shepherd. They can't *really* be worse than he is, even if they *are* Jews.'

Half-hidden in the shadow of the trees, Elvira made an angry face at him. But Benedict shook his head urgently.

'Not a word,' he whispered. 'We *mustn't* take any part in this. We mustn't give ourselves away.'

The clip-clop of horses' hoofs could now be heard echoing through the green silence of the forest. Then came voices – a deep voice followed by lighter, younger tones. The outlaws were silent, waiting in a ring for their prey, their hands on their daggers.

49

Benedict and Elvira crouched well back in the shadow of the thicket, also waiting . . .

And now they could see the two Jewish merchants through a gap in the trees. They rode on fine black horses and wore rich, fur-trimmed gowns – an old man with a thick grey beard, and a younger man with black hair and flashing dark eyes. The older man, thought Elvira, looked like Uncle Hugo – Uncle Hugo who had died in Lymford. They were the first Jews she had seen since she and Benedict had begun their journey, and a wave of homesickness swept over her.

The Jews rode unsuspectingly into the glade, and then reined abruptly as they saw the reception that awaited them.

'Don't be afraid, gentlemen,' said Robin Hood soothingly, holding aloft his dagger so that its silver blade sparkled in the sunlight. 'All we want is fifty gold pieces from each of you, to help ransom our Lord the King. As loyal subjects, you will not refuse your help.'

The old man began to unfasten his saddle-bag with trembling fingers. But his young companion angrily refastened the bag, and then stared back at Robin defiantly.

'As loyal subjects,' he replied, 'we have already contributed to the King's ransom.'

'Ssssh, Daniel . . .' whispered the old man anxiously, but Robin broke in with a polite smile.

'Seeing that you Jews have most to gain from the King's return,' he said, 'I would have thought you would be happy to give a little extra to help bring him home.'

'We *have* given extra . . . twice as much as any Norman lord,' said Daniel hotly. 'We Jews are taxed and robbed almost out of existence. You called us citizens, but we are not. We are only the king's money-bags.'

Little John, his face as red as his hair, lunged forward angrily and brandished his staff above the old man's head.

'Do you dare imply,' he thundered, 'that our king is a thief? I'll show you unbelieving Jews who . . .'

But he did not finish his threat. For, at that moment, Elvira ran out of the thicket and twined her arms about the old man's waist.

'Don't hurt him,' she cried. 'Please don't hurt him. He looks like my Uncle Hugo.'

Little John, his staff suspended in mid-air, looked down at her in amazement. Elvira saw his face, and looked about her at the astounded faces of the other Outlaws. Then she realised what she had done.

'*He* looks like your uncle?' echoed Little John, pointing his staff at the old merchant.

'A little bit like him,' faltered Elvira. 'Not very much.'

For a few moments nobody spoke. Silence hung so heavy in the forest that Elvira could hear the leaves rustle. She no longer saw the faces of the Outlaws; they had turned into a circle of vague blurs. She was aware only of the old man's frightened brown eyes under his yellow cap, of the mystified face of the younger merchant, and of Benedict's face, pale and tense, staring at her out of the thicket.

'I have betrayed us,' she thought in despair. 'After all this time, I have given away our secret. And now they will kill us.'

Robin Hood looked at Elvira for a moment, and then turned to look at Benedict. Then he sheathed his dagger, stepped forward, and held out his hand to the old merchant.

'Sir, you must forgive our haste,' he said. 'I quite understand that you have already contributed to our

King's ransom. We shall not bother you any more.'

Little John looked as though he were about to explode.

'B-but you're not going to let them go without giving us anything, are you?' he spluttered. 'They can afford it.'

'We are not barbarians,' replied Robin sternly. 'Will, Alan, escort these gentlemen out of the forest. And see that they leave Sherwood unmolested.'

After the two merchants had gone, both thanking Robin warmly and promising to remember him in their prayers, Friar Tuck scratched his bald pate with a puzzled air.

'I'm afraid I still don't understand, Robin,' he said politely.

'And nor do I,' growled Little John.

'Don't you?' replied Robin, with a little smile.

He walked slowly towards the children, who were huddled together in the thicket.

'I should have guessed,' he said, taking Elvira's face gently in both his hands and gazing at it. 'I should have known you were neither Norman nor Saxon.'

'D-do you mean that *they* . . .?' began Friar Tuck in astonishment.

Elvira wriggled out of Robin's grasp and began to run towards the edge of the clearing, but Robin gripped her skirt and hauled her back, laughing.

'There's no need for that,' he said. 'You – boy, come here, and sit on this log.'

Benedict, quaking inwardly, seated himself on the mossy wood. Robin Hood placed the still trembling Elvira beside him, and then knelt down so that his face was on a level with theirs.

'And now,' he said in a gentle voice, 'suppose you tell me all about it?'

CHAPTER 6

The Quest Begins

SIR Edward de Bourg rode into Sherwood Forest next day, his white surcoat gleaming in the sun and his spurs and bridle bells jingling.

Benedict and Elvira met him at supper that evening, and they were overwhelmed by his splendour. Overwhelmed . . . and a little frightened. They remembered watching once from the window of Father's study as a procession of Crusader knights had passed through Lymford from York on its way to the wars. And now the sight of Sir Edward's tall white-clad figure with the scarlet cross blazing on its breast brought back Father's words. 'These are our deadliest enemies,' he had said as the brilliant array of horsemen, armour glittering and pennants flying, had clattered over the cobbled street below, 'because they believe they are fighting a holy war. To them, we Jews are not human beings; we are only the anti-Christ. Their mission in life is to destroy us.'

Remembering this, the children took care to keep well out of range of Sir Edward's keen grey eyes. They had already been briefly introduced to him as two

run-away apprentices; now they hovered on the edge
of the group at supper, eating their bread and cheese
in a dark corner, and listening quietly to the gay
chatter and singing and laughter.

Once or twice, though, Elvira found herself stealing
a sly glance at the Crusader. He was certainly very
handsome, she thought, and there was a humorous
twinkle in his eyes. 'I wish we could be friends,' she
said to herself a little wistfully. 'He looks as though
he could be kind, even if he *is* a Crusader. Still I
don't suppose we shall ever have the chance to find
out.'

Long after the children had crawled into the pile
of rabbit-skins that was their bed, the feasting and
revelry went on in Sherwood. The huge venison pasty
was eaten to the last crumb, and toasts were drunk to
the King's health and to the success of Sir Edward's
mission. Robin Hood and his Outlaws were loyal sup-
porters of King Richard, and Sir Edward was the
most popular guest those green glades had ever known.

The gaiety and good cheer continued all next morning. But when the children met Sir Edward and the
Outlaws again at dinner, they realised that something
had gone wrong. Faces looked grim and tense; conversation seemed forced, and Friar Tuck was the only
person who showed any appetite. And not a single
toast was drunk to the King's ransom.

'Have they quarrelled, I wonder?' thought Benedict. '*Something* has happened; I wish I knew what.'

He was to know soon enough. When dinner at last
came to an end, Robin Hood came slowly to where
Benedict and Elvira were sitting.

'I should like to speak to you children alone,' he
said, and his expression was grave.

As they followed Robin to the glade which was his
special sanctum, both children felt their hearts

sinking.

'I suppose he's going to tell us that we've outstayed our welcome,' thought Benedict. 'He's forgiven us for being Jewish but he thinks it's time we moved on.' And Elvira, who was thinking much the same thoughts, realised that there were tears in her eyes. She and Benedict had always known that they could not stay in Sherwood for ever, but she did not want to leave yet. Not just yet.

But now they were in Robin's special glade. He motioned the children to sit on the grass, and then sat down beside them.

For a few moments there was silence. Then Robin cleared his throat.

'I have called you here,' he said at last, 'because I need your help. In fact, we *all* need your help.'

If the children had not been sitting on the grass they would almost certainly have collapsed with shock. Their eyes and mouths fell open. 'We all need your help,' Robin had said. He had actually said it. But what did he mean, and why did he look so solemn?

Robin looked at the two astonished little faces, and smiled faintly.

'You know, of course, why Sir Edward has come to Sherwood,' he said. 'What you may *not* know is that there are certain people who would not be glad to see King Richard return from captivity. Barons, for example, who grow more and more powerful when the King is away. Toadies who have been making themselves popular with Prince John, and would like to see *him* on the throne. Some of these people would do anything to prevent the ransom money from reaching the Queen.'

The children looked back at Robin gravely. They knew all this already. They had heard Father discussing it with Uncle Hugo. But they did not understand how it concerned them.

'When I say they would do anything,' added Robin, 'I mean *anything*. Even murder. It could come to that. In fact, it *has* come to that.'

What did he mean? thought the children. Sir Edward was alive and well. They had seen him at dinner only a few minutes ago.

'Sir Edward is in great danger,' said Robin, as though in answer to their thoughts. 'Tom was drinking in a tavern near Nottingham this morning. He overheard some of Prince John's followers plotting to waylay Sir Edward on the road to London, and kill him.'

Elvira gasped. Already, in her mind's eye, she could see the handsome Sir Edward lying dead by the roadside, his dazzling surcoat all streaked with dust and blood. But Benedict was more practical. Robin, he thought, must have a reason for telling them this.

'Is there something *we* can do to help, sir?' he asked politely.

Robin smiled.

'There is,' he replied. 'It involves a little game of make-believe.'

The children looked at him in bewilderment.

'We have had a long discussion,' said Robin, 'and it seems to us that Sir Edward will have to travel in disguise if he is to reach London safely. Disguised to look as ordinary as possible. As a merchant, for example. Going to London to visit a sick old mother.'

'That sounds a good idea,' said Benedict approvingly – though Elvira secretly thought that Sir Edward, even disguised as a merchant, could never look ordinary.

'I'm glad you think so,' replied Robin. 'But we want to make his disguise as convincing as possible. And a family man looks more convincing if he has a family.'

A child or two . . .'

And then both children understood why Robin had called them into his sanctum.

'Us?' said Benedict.

Robin nodded.

'You will go with him to London, and stay with him till the ransom money has been handed to the Queen. Then he will see to it that you reach Oxford safely. All this, of course, if you agree.'

'But why *shouldn't* we agree?' squealed Elvira, thinking that this would surely be the most exciting game she and Benedict had ever played. 'It sounds fun.'

Robin leaned forward and grasped her hand.

'But it *isn't* fun, sweetheart,' he said urgently. 'You must understand, before you agree to anything. It really isn't a game, believe me. I can't let you do this unless you understand that it isn't a game.'

Elvira looked at him in surprise.

'Sir Edward's enemies are ruthless men,' added Robin. 'If they found him out, they would stop at nothing.'

'W-would they kill *us* too?' faltered Benedict.

Robin paused, and then nodded.

For a few moments there was silence. The golden afternoon light filtering through the tree-tops, thought Benedict, made Elvira's face look quite yellow. She was looking at him with wide, dark eyes, as she had looked that last evening in Lymford. His own hands were numb and cold. Had he and Elvira escaped death, only to meet it in a different guise?

'I don't want to persuade you,' Robin went on. 'I should hate to send you into any more danger. You've suffered enough already. But I wonder if you realise what this would mean to *your* people?'

'I don't understand,' said Benedict, swallowing hard.

'Then let me try to explain. *We* want to ransom King Richard because he's our true King. And because we admire him. He's strong and brave and chivalrous . . . we admire all that. But for you Jews he's something more. He's your natural protector.'

'P-protector?'

'Against the Barons. While the King is at home, there's order in the land. The Barons are afraid of him. But Prince John, *he* lets the Barons do as they please. Let them behave as they please, and the first thing they do is murder and plunder the Jews. Well, I don't have to tell you. You saw that for yourselves, didn't you?'

'Yes, we did,' said Benedict quietly, remembering how Henry de Poulny, his dark face ablaze, had urged the mob forward in the market square at Lymford.

'Most of the Barons owe money to the Jews,' Robin went on. 'And death is the easiest way to cancel a debt.'

Memories, strange and disjointed, were coming back to Benedict as Robin spoke. Father, remarking that Henry de Poulny would stop at nothing to wipe out his debts. Alaric the mercer, on Lymford's night of death, describing the burning of the deeds in the market-place and adding 'The King will be angry when he comes home.' And Robin himself, only a few days ago, demanding money from the Jewish merchants with the words 'Seeing that you Jews have most to gain from the King's return, I would have thought you would be happy to give a little extra to help bring him home . . .'

Perhaps, thought Benedict, he and Elvira had been saved from the massacre for a purpose. Perhaps they were the instruments chosen by God to help save the rest of the Jews of England.

'*I'm* willing, sir,' he said bravely, surprised to find

that his voice was still wobbly. 'But it depends on Elvira.'

Robin turned to Elvira, who was looking thoughtful.

'Well?' he said gently.

Elvira closed her eyes, gulped – then opened them and looked at him steadily.

'It was awful, what happened in Lymford,' she said. 'We mustn't let it happen again.'

Robin lifted Elvira and swung her high in the air.

'I knew you would agree,' he said happily, while Benedict stared at his sister in astonishment. 'You're brave children, both of you. I never knew Jews could be so brave.'

And strangely enough, Benedict, who up till that moment had been trembling with fear, *did* feel brave now. Perhaps it was the thought of being the saviour of his people. Perhaps it was because the decision was made and there was no going back. He glanced at Elvira, and saw that she was smiling.

That evening, Robin told Sir Edward that the children had agreed to go with him to London. Sir Edward smiled and thanked them, but did not say very much more. The mission had to be planned out in great detail, and he and Robin had a lot to discuss.

'Sir Edward is going to travel to London as Master William Holyard, cloth merchant, of the city of York,' Robin told the children next morning. 'You two can keep your assumed names. John and Alice Holyard sounds just right. We'll have to get some new clothes for the three of you. We can't have a city merchant's children travelling in rags like those, and Sir Edward certainly can't travel in Crusader dress.'

'There's something else I wanted to ask you sir,' said Benedict, feeling a little embarrassed. 'Sir Edward doesn't know we're Jewish. You told him that story

... about us being apprentices ... remember? Do you think we ought to tell him the truth?'

Robin looked a little worried.

'Sir Edward is a good man,' he said, 'but he's a Crusader, and the Crusaders have never felt particularly friendly towards the Jews. If I were you, I should say nothing.'

So, when they were alone, Benedict warned Elvira very solemnly that she must keep a strict guard on her tongue. And she assured him, just as solemnly, that she would.

'It's a pity, though,' she added. 'He's such a nice, handsome man – I wish he *didn't* hate Jews.'

The next few days passed quickly. Somehow or other the Outlaws acquired new clothes for the three travellers ... plain but expensive garments, the kind a prosperous merchant and his children would wear. When Benedict and Elvira saw Sir Edward for the first time in his disguise, they did not recognise him. He had shaved off his beard, and in his dark woollen tunic and sober green cloak he looked quite different ... dignified still, but not nearly so awe-inspiring.

'So this is my family!' he said cheerfully, chucking Elvira under the chin. 'It's a pity we're strangers, but we shall know each other better by the end of the journey.'

'Not *too* well, I hope,' thought Benedict, but he smiled back dutifully. The idea of calling this Jew-hating stranger 'Father' did not really appeal to him. The image of Simon the Physician was still vivid in his thoughts, no matter how hard he tried to forget.

But Elvira was completely charmed by the Crusader. She helped him pack a huge saddle-bag with food for the journey, meat-pies and hard-boiled eggs and cheese and fruit, keeping up a constant chatter as she worked.

At last everything was ready, and the horses stood saddled and waiting. Elvira was to ride pillion behind Sir Edward, and Benedict was to have the fine chestnut that had belonged to Henry Shepherd.

'It's a gentle beast,' Will Scarlett assured him. 'Even though you haven't had much riding practice you'll be able to hang on. Oh, *we're* very particular about the horses we steal, I can tell you.'

It was not till they were in the saddle, with the Outlaws crowding about them to say goodbye, that the children remembered again that they were going on a dangerous quest and might never see the end of it. Suddenly they felt very small and lonely. Sherwood Forest was home now, and Robin and his Outlaws had taken the place of their lost family.

'I don't want to leave you,' sobbed Elvira, clinging to Friar Tuck, who was her special favourite.

'Oh, I'm sure we shall meet again,' replied Friar Tuck consolingly. 'I feel it in my bones.' And he gave his huge paunch a resounding slap, making Elvira laugh through her tears.

'If anything goes wrong,' said Robin Hood to Sir Edward, 'if you should find yourself in any danger, try to get a message through to us. Do your best. Remember.'

Then he escorted the travellers to the edge of the forest and stood waving goodbye till the sound of the horses' hoofs had died away. As for the children, they looked back and waved and waved till Sherwood was only a dark green streak on the misty horizon, and then not even that. And then they turned their faces resolutely towards the long and dusty road that curved over the hills to London.

Recognition

IT was, thought Elvira, very much better than walking. The horses were pounding on so fast over the scarred and rutted road that she would not be surprised if they reached London by nightfall.

Balanced comfortably on the pillion, her arms clasped tightly about Sir Edward's waist and her cheek resting against his broad, woollen back, she listened drowsily as he talked about the capital and all its marvels and the wonderful time they would have there when their mission was fulfilled.

Benedict, clinging nervously to the bridle of his gentle chestnut, did not feel quite so happy. Every bump and furrow in the road jerked him almost out of the saddle, and he was beginning to wish he had had more riding practice. Hebrew and Latin, botany and astrology were all very well, but there were times when a man also needed to be able to keep his seat on a horse.

'I'm just not cut out to be a man of action,' he thought. 'Or a hero. It's a good thing I'm going to be a physician when I grow up. Sitting in a stuffy old surgery looking at people's warts is just about all I'm fit for.'

Much to Elvira's disappointment, they did *not* reach their destination that evening. The fiery light of sunset found them riding into a small village called Candleford, about four miles, so Sir Edward told them, from Nottingham.

'I thought we were nearly in London,' said Elvira plaintively.

'*London?*' gasped Sir Edward, and he roared with laughter. 'We've a good week of travelling yet, my poppet. To get from Sherwood to London in one day a man would have to be able to fly, and you can be sure *that* will never happen.'

Benedict was trying not to look as dismayed as he felt. 'Another week?' he thought. 'A week of wobbling about in the saddle, guarding my tongue, and making excuses for not eating meat? I can't stand it. I shall die . . .'

A pig came waddling across the road at this moment, and Benedict reined so sharply that he almost fell off his horse.

'Steady,' said Sir Edward with a smile. 'Wait till the ostler helps you dismount. There's an inn just down the road, and I thought we might spend the night there. I only hope the rats and fleas will leave some sleeping-space for *us*.'

'R-rats? F-fleas?' faltered Elvira, while Benedict steadied himself in the saddle and tried to look dignified.

'Most of these inns are stinking old holes,' replied Sir Edward cheerfully. 'I've stayed in plenty, and I should know. In one I had to share a bed with a drunken tinker *and* all his pots and pans. In another the rats ate my mattress during the night. There wasn't a scrap left by morning. But I don't suppose *this* inn will be any worse than most.'

And with these encouraging words he brought his horse to a halt outside a large stone house with a bush, which was the sign of an alehouse, at its door. Peat smoke poured in a black column from a hole in the roof; the sound of ribald singing came from the darkness beyond the open door, and – as the travellers watched – a drunken man, still clasping his empty tankard, came staggering and hiccuping out of the inn and fell flat on his face in the gutter.

'Well, at least that proves their liquor is good and strong,' said Sir Edward gaily. 'Are you a drinking man, John?'

'I like mead, sir,' replied Benedict with dignity.

'Mead? Your master shoemaker must have spoiled you,' laughed Sir Edward. 'I thought he never gave you anything but dry crusts and water.'

Elvira glanced nervously at Benedict, but at that moment a fat ostler appeared from the stable and came towards them, his arms outstretched in welcome.

'Greetings, my master,' he cried, gathering the horses' reins in his huge leathery hands. Are you going to do us the honour of spending the night here? We've some fine company. There's Master Shepherd and Master Ridley . . .'

'We can do without the company,' said Sir Edward. 'All we want is a room for the night. These children are tired. Can you give us a room to ourselves?'

'I believe there *is* an empty room, sir,' said the ostler, and Elvira, who had been hoping there would be no drunken tinkers at *this* inn, sighed with relief.

The travellers dismounted, and the ostler took their horses to the stable, promising to give them plenty of oats and good fresh water. Sir Edward, meanwhile, shepherded the children into the inn. He looked as calm and confident as ever, and Benedict and Elvira could not guess that he was inwardly as nervous as they were.

The inn was dark and smoky, lit only by a few rush-lights and the peat fire that choked and spluttered in the middle of the room, and the walls were covered with grotesque, dancing shadows. The rushes that strewed the ground were matted with scraps of food and old, chewed bones, and half a dozen mangy cats and dogs were rolling about on the floor, fighting each other for choice morsels.

'At least there won't be any rats here,' thought Elvira, glancing nervously at the threshing bodies. 'But there *might* be fleas. Dogs have fleas, don't they?'

'It's not exactly a palace, is it?' whispered Sir Edward. 'Never mind, we'll try to find a monastery for tomorrow night. Monasteries make the best inns. There's a bit too much praying for my taste, but the beds are clean.'

A group of gruff-looking peasants, drinking and bawling out their songs in a corner of the room, glanced up at the newcomers before burying their faces in their tankards again. But the two well-dressed men who were sitting together in another corner did not even notice the travellers; they were too engrossed in earnest conversation. Benedict heard one of them, a fat, pompous-looking gentleman, say 'Yes, a giant of a fellow with red hair. I gave *him* a thrashing he won't forget in a hurry.' And the other man nodded, obviously deeply impressed.

At this moment the landlord, who had been hovering about the pompous-looking gentleman with a dish of sweetmeats, caught sight of Sir Edward and the children and came hurrying to greet them.

'A room for the night, sir?' he said. 'Yes, we have one. A gentleman died there last night. But don't worry; its been well aired. And now, what would you

like to eat? There's sucking-pig and trout and capons
. . . we've the best of everything in this house!'

Sir Edward ordered the sucking-pig for himself and
some broiled trout for the children, and the landlord
told a fat serving-maid, who had been gazing
admiringly at Sir Edward, to hurry to the kitchen
and see the food prepared. Then he showed the
travellers into the secluded corner where the two well-
dressed gentlemen were sitting, and yelled at a serving-
lad to bring a seat for Sir Edward.

The pompous-looking gentleman, who had been
saying something to his companions about 'a lot of
rogues and thieves who don't dare show their faces
among honest men,' looked up at the strangers without much enthusiasm.

'Sir,' said the landlord with a polite little bow, 'may
I present Master Shepherd and Master Ridley? They
are distinguished gentlemen in these parts. Master
Shepherd and Master Ridley, may I present . . .?'
And he looked enquiringly at Sir Edward.

'William Holyard, cloth merchant, of the city of
York,' said Sir Edward. 'Sirs, I am glad to make your
acquaintance. May I present my son, John, and my
daughter, Alice?' Benedict gave a little bow and Elvira
curtseyed, and both gentlemen nodded back gravely.

Here the serving-lad appeared, staggering under the
weight of a great wooden chair, and the pompous
gentleman raised his eyebrows. Chairs were reserved
only for honoured guests; everyone else sat on benches
or on the floor, and he was annoyed at the deference
being shown to the newcomer.

'Are you taking a business trip, sir?' he said coldly, as
Sir Edward seated himself comfortably in the big chair.

'A private journey,' replied Sir Edward. 'We are
travelling to London to visit my mother. She is over
seventy, and has been in bad health lately.'

'Ah, they don't last long once they get to that age,' said Master Ridley, who was long and thin, with a pale, doleful face.

'I hope God will preserve her for many years,' replied Sir Edward, trying to look shocked and anxious. 'Sit down, children, and make yourselve comfortable. Our supper is coming.'

The children squatted on the floor at Sir Edward's feet and thought hungrily of the trout being cooked in the kitchen. Elvira looked up shyly into Master Shepherd's peevish face and decided that she did not like it very much. Then she began to wonder where she had heard the name 'Shepherd' before.

'You didn't happen to pass through Sherwood Forest, did you?' said Master Shepherd suddenly.

Sir Edward started, and tried to cover his confusion with a burst of coughing.

'That's a nasty cough, Master Holyard,' observed Master Ridley sadly. 'A friend of mine once started to cough like that, and within a year he was dead.'

Sir Edward mopped his streaming eyes, and turned to Master Shepherd.

'I can't *remember* passing through Sherwood,' he replied slowly. 'Why do you ask?'

'There's a gang of thieves living there,' replied the pompous man with a smug little smile. 'Robin Hood and his merry men. *I* beat them up a fortnight ago. The whole bunch of them.'

'You did? Incredible,' said Sir Edward, meaning it.

'Yes, I beat them all up,' added Master Shepherd with slow satisfaction. 'They were trying to rob me, but they didn't get far, *I* can tell you. There was one red-haired fellow who was ten feet tall. I gave *him* a thrashing he won't forget in a hurry.'

Sir Edward thought of Little John's powerful muscles, and smiled.

'*We've* had an uneventful journey so far, haven't we, children?' he said, a tinge of regret in his voice. 'But then, we always do. No one expects a cloth merchant to have adventures.'

Master Shepherd glanced at Sir Edward coldly. Then he looked at him again with a little more interest.

'You know, I'm sure I've seen you before,' he said. 'I can't think where, but I never forget a face.'

'It's quite possible,' said Sir Edward, trying to look calm though his heart was thumping uncomfortably. 'Have you ever been to York?'

'No,' replied Master Shepherd. 'Have *you* ever been to Sudwell?'

'I don't think I've ever heard of it.'

'*I* live there,' snapped Master Shepherd. 'I'm very highly thought of in those parts.'

Sir Edward was beginning to feel a sinking in his stomach. He *had* visited Sudwell; he remembered it now. He had been in Sudwell less than three weeks ago, collecting tax for King Richard's ransom. He must have called on Master Shepherd for money. And now Master Shepherd might recognise him at any moment.

Elvira, who was resting against Sir Edward's knee, felt it tremble.

'Now don't tell me,' Master Shepherd went on, and he took a deep draught of wine, then screwed up his little piggy eyes and examined Sir Edward narrowly. 'I'll have it in a moment. I never forget a face. Though, mind you, I could swear you had a beard when I saw you last. A dark beard. Now *where* was it we met?'

Benedict looked at Master Shepherd, and thought how cruel his mouth was. Then he turned to glance at Elvira, who was very pale. 'I feel sick,' she thought to herself. 'If this goes on, I shall *be* sick.' And then she had an idea.

'Are you *sure* you've never been to Sudwell?' said Master Shepherd again, gazing intently into Sir Edward's face.

But Sir Edward did not have to reply. For all at once Elvira sprang up and buried her face in his lap. 'I feel sick, Father,' she moaned. 'I think I'm going to be ill. Very ill.'

For a moment Sir Edward believed her, and was anxious. Then she raised her face a fraction and gave him a little smile, and he understood.

'My poor little girl!' he said anxiously, lifting her tenderly in his arms. 'Have you got a pain?'

'Yes, lots of pains. One in my head, and one in my stomach, and one in my . . . er . . . in my arm. Ooh!' Elvira groaned again very loudly, and Benedict looked up at her admiringly.

'I wish *I* could have thought of something like that,' he said to himself. 'She's quite clever sometimes, even though she's a girl.'

Their companions, meanwhile, were looking very alarmed. Master Shepherd had stopped trying to identify Sir Edward and now began to edge away from Elvira, muttering something about the plague. Master Ridley, his long white face more doleful than ever, launched into the story of a little girl he had known who had been taken ill in exactly the same way, and had died in terrible agonies. The peasants stopped singing and put their tankards down on the table, grateful for a little excitement. And the landlord came running, red-faced and anxious, to ask if he should call a physician.

'No, I'm sure it's nothing,' said Sir Edward hastily. 'She's been on horseback all day, and she's a bad traveller. All she wants is her bed. A night's sleep will do her more good than any medicine.'

'I'm tired too, Father,' said Benedict eagerly, and Sir Edward turned and gave him a slow wink.

'If you're *sure* it's not the plague,' said Master Shepherd grudgingly.

'She's always like this when she's over-tired,' said Sir Edward, and he lifted Elvira's limp body in his arms. 'If you will forgive us, sirs, we will go to our room.'

'But your supper . . .' said the poor, flustered landlord. 'It's being prepared in the kitchen; it's nearly ready . . .'

'We'll have it upstairs,' replied Sir Edward. 'I also feel tired and sick. We've had a long, hard journey. Good night, gentlemen. It was a pleasure to meet you.'

'I'll get Betsy to see you to your room,' said the landlord. 'There's a hole in the stairs; mind you don't fall through it.'

After Sir Edward and the children, Elvira still writhing and groaning, had been escorted upstairs by the fat serving-maid, Master Shepherd gulped his wine sulkily and turned to his companion.

'That fellow!' he snorted. 'Bringing his disease-ridden children here among decent folk. It will serve him right if she *has* got the plague and we all die of it. I never liked him from the beginning.'

'Why not?' said Master Ridley in surprise. 'He seems a very nice gentleman.'

'Too full of his own importance,' snapped Master Shepherd. 'Expected to be waited on like a King. He's got no right to be so smug; I dare say you and I could buy him up ten times over. I hate these proud no-bodies. Pride is the greatest of all sins, *I* always say.'

'Quite right, too,' agreed Master Ridley.

'The greatest of *all* sins. By the way, Tom, did I

tell you how I thrashed Robin Hood the other day?'

'You did.'

Master Shepherd shrugged his shoulders.

'Ah well,' he sighed, 'I suppose I'd better go to the stable and see how my horse is getting on. Well-bred sensitive creatures like mine get nervous if they're left alone too long.'

He rose heavily from his chair and waddled pompously out into the dark courtyard, not altogether sorry to be free of Master Ridley's company. 'He's a fool,' he thought contemptuously. 'Didn't seem the least bit excited when I told him about Robin Hood. Hasn't a spark of feeling in him. And as for that merchant, Holyard, or whatever his name is, I've never come across a more conceited upstart in my life.'

His horse whinneyed as he entered the stable, and he approached the stall and patted its soft nose.

'Were you lonely, my beauty?' he said. 'Have you got nice friends here? There are two more horses, I see. Have you been talking to them?'

The fine, sleek chestnut in the next stall, he thought, looked very familiar. He looked at it with interest. Then his eyes bulged, and he looked again.

Swallowing hard, he lifted the horse's leg and peered at the fetlock. The stable was dimly lit, but he could just make out what he had expected to see. His own mark branded into the soft, dark skin.

Master Ridley was half-dozing by the fire when his friend came storming back into the inn. The latter's face was pale with rage, and Master Ridley sat bolt upright, the landlord came running in panic, and the peasants set down their tankards again and watched to see what new entertainment was forthcoming.

'Those three upstairs!' spluttered Master Shepherd, pointing furiously towards the ceiling. 'That fine merchant, Master Holyard . . . he's stolen my horse!'

'D-do you mean to say your horse is g-gone, sir?' said the landlord, turning very pale.

'Not *that* one, you idiot!' shrieked Master Shepherd. 'I mean the other one. The one that was stolen from me by Robin Hood.'

'I'm afraid I don't understand, sir,' faltered the poor landlord.

'It's clear enough to anyone with a grain of intelligence! What I mean is that one of the horses lodged in your stable by your precious Master Holyard is the very horse that was stolen from me in Sherwood Forest two weeks ago. Do you understand now, numskull?'

The landlord gazed at him open-mouthed.

'Then h-how did it come into Master Holyard's possession?' he quavered.

'That's what I intend to find out. You must send for the Sheriff of Nottingham at once, and have this prince of cloth merchants arrested.'

Master Ridley's eyes opened wide in dismay.

'That's a bit hard, isn't it?' he said. 'Couldn't you have it out with him yourself?'

'What? With a horse-thief and an accomplice of Robin Hood? No, he shall suffer, or my name's not Henry Shepherd. Landlord, will you send your boy to Nottingham to summon the Sheriff's men, or shall I report you for harbouring criminals?'

'I-I shall see to it at once, sir,' faltered the landlord, and he went to call his serving-lad, while the furious Henry Shepherd slopped back onto his bench muttering something about 'vengeance' and 'pompous upstarts.'

A few minutes later, the dark silence of the courtyard was broken by the clatter of hoofs. The serving-lad wrapped his cloak round him to keep out the chill night air, and spurred his horse towards Nottingham.

CHAPTER 8

The Menorah
of Maxenburg

'I REALLY thought he had us that time,' said Sir Edward, and he crammed a morsel of roast pork into his mouth and licked his fingers appreciatively. 'That was quick thinking on your part, Alice. Another ten seconds, and old pot-belly would have recognised me.'

Elvira flushed happily.

'It was nothing,' she said modestly. 'Besides, I really *did* feel a bit sick.'

'And so did I,' added Benedict, who was diligently finishing up what was left of the broiled trout.

'You'll be sick now, if you weren't sick then,' said Sir Edward reprovingly. 'What would Friar Tuck say if he saw you gobbling like that? Would you like a bit of pork to finish with?'

He held out a choice tit-bit to Benedict, who recoiled.

'N-no thank you, sir,' he replied hastily. 'I've had enough.'

Supper was nearly over in the attic room assigned to the travellers, and they were now beginning to feel pleasantly sleepy. Sleepy and safe. It was not exactly a luxurious room. It was damp and cold; the heavy stone walls were bare and had a faintly mossy smell, and the rushlight flung a pool of pallid light into the centre of the floor, leaving the corners dark and mysterious. But there was something reassuring about those frowning stone walls, and about the heavy door that shut away the outside world . . . and Master Shepherd.

'That nasty man nearly found us out,' thought Elvira, and a little shiver ran down her spine. 'But he can't harm us now. We're safe.'

Benedict, though, did not feel quite so happy. It was not fear of discovery by Master Shepherd that worried him now. It was fear of discovery by Sir Edward.

'If he knew we were Jewish,' he thought, as he watched Sir Edward hacking up the remains of the sucking-pig with a wicked-looking dagger, 'there's no knowing what he might do to us. And we keep *nearly* giving ourselves away. Every conversation we have could lead to something. Elvira especially. She gets chattering to him and she forgets to think. We'll *have* to be more careful.'

'Have an apricot,' said Sir Edward amiably, hand-ing him a dish of candied fruit, and Benedict stopped worrying for the moment.

The apricots were soon gone, and Elvira, who had quite forgotten her tiredness, began to look round the bleak room for some other source of amusement. But all she could find was Sir Edward's luggage . . . three saddlebags, one containing food and money for the journey, one crammed with the gold that was King Richard's ransom, and the third a great bulging, knobbly bag of battered leather.

'What's in here?' she asked, prodding the bumps with an inquisitive finger.

'Alice, that's not very polite,' said Benedict reprovingly, but Sir Edward laughed.

'I've no idea,' he replied. 'That's one of the saddlebags I use when I go to the Crusades. I haven't even unpacked it; as soon as I arrived home from Europe I was given this ransom mission, and I picked up my bag and was away. I was a fool not to empty it, really; it's horribly heavy. There could be *anything* inside.'

'Can I see?' said Elvira eagerly. 'Can I unpack it for you?'

'It doesn't really need to be unpacked,' replied Sir Edward. Then, seeing Elvira's face fall, he added kindly, 'All right, poppet, you can if you like. But put everything back again neatly.'

'Oh, I will. Isn't this exciting?' And Elvira began to force apart the clasps of the bag, while Sir Edward looked on indulgently.

'If you find any liquor in there, you can give it to me,' he said. 'And if you find any sweetmeats, *you* can have them. There, that's a promise. Though they'll be a bit dusty by now.'

Elvira closed her eyes blissfully, plunged her arm deep into the bag, and brought out a grimy-looking goatskin flagon.

'I do believe she's made an important discovery,' exclaimed Sir Edward in delight, and he took the flagon, unscrewed it, and sniffed at the contents.

'Yes, it's a flagon of the best French wine,' he said. 'I didn't know I had any left. There, aren't I lucky?'

'Yes, and aren't you glad you let me unpack your bag?' squealed Elvira. 'Now I'll try to find something for John. And then perhaps a doll for me.'

'Here, I'm not the keeper of the King's treasury,' protested Sir Edward, while Benedict sat back on his heels and roared with laughter.

Elvira delved again into the bag, and this time came

up with a book, bound in leather and tooled with gold.

'Do you want this?' she said, holding it out to Sir Edward. But he was too deeply engrossed in the French wine to reply.

Benedict, who loved books, took it eagerly and began to flick through the pages, which were beautifully illuminated with leaves and flowers and tiny exquisite pictures in green and blue and amethyst, dazzling crimson and gold.

'It's a Bible,' he said. 'A Latin Bible.'

'Oh yes, I always take that with me when I go to the Crusades,' replied Sir Edward idly. 'It impresses the heathen.'

Benedict turned over a few more pages, and then looked up, puzzled.

'It's got the Old Testament in it', he said.

'Of course. Why shouldn't it have the Old Testament in it?'

'I just didn't think yours would,' said Benedict, quite forgetting to be careful.

'Why, doesn't *yours*?'

'No . . . er . . . yes,' stammered Benedict, suddenly realising what he had said. But Sir Edward's thoughts, luckily, seemed to be elsewhere.

'I like the Old Testament,' he said suddenly, 'Especially the Psalms.' And then, to the children's surprise, he began to quote Psalm 121.

'I will lift up mine eyes to the hills,
Whence cometh my help.
My help cometh from the Lord,
Which made Heaven and Earth.
He will not suffer they foot to be moved;
He that guardeth thee will not slumber.
Behold, He that guardeth Israel with neither
          slumber nor sleep . . .'

The beautiful words floated into the silence like birds into a still sky, and suddenly the whole room seemed, to Benedict, to be changed. He was not in the dingy attic any longer; he was in Father's study, with its crimson velvet hangings, and the gold Menorah burned on the mother-of-pearl table like a living flame. News of the massacre had just come from York, and Father, pale and shaken himself, yet trying to calm his terrified family, was reciting the words which always seemed to him to have the greatest healing power. But the words were Hebrew, not English.

'Eso enai el heharim me-ayin yavo ezri.
Ezri me-im adonai osei, shomayim va-aretz...'

Benedict was not aware, at first, that he had spoken them aloud. In any case, what did it matter? He was safe at home, with his family, in the red and gold room. And then he looked up, and the spell was broken. He saw the dark stone walls of the attic, and Sir Edward looking at him in surprise, and Elvira wide-eyed in horror and apprehension, and the Hebrew he was chanting died away into silence.

'What's that you're muttering, my boy?' said Sir Edward amiably.

'Er . . . I was just . . . just reciting the Psalm,' stuttered Benedict, aware that Elvira had clapped her hand over her mouth as though to stifle a scream.

'Were you? Didn't sound like it. It sounded like a lot of nonsense,' replied Sir Edward. 'You're tired out, that's *your* trouble.' And he stretched himself, and gave a huge yawn.

Benedict felt his legs buckle in terror and relief. Sweat ran down his forehead, and he did not dare look at Elvira again. 'I keep blaming *her* for talking too much,' he thought miserably, 'but I'm much worse. I keep forgetting where I am. Perhaps I *am* tired out. I think perhaps I'd better go to bed before I do any real damage.'

Sir Edward yawned again.

'Have you nearly finished unpacking, poppet?' he said to Elvira. 'I think we ought to sleep now, but I'd love to know if there's any more wine in that bag.'

'I'll look,' said Elvira quickly.

There *was* another flask of wine, Rhenish, this time, and Sir Edward greeted it with enthusiasm.

'I like to collect souvenirs from all the countries I visit,' he told the children, 'and it's usually liquor. There should be some wine from the Holy Land too. It's probably right at the bottom of the bag.'

'The *Holy* Land? Have you really been *there*?' And Elvira gazed at Sir Edward with sparkling eyes.

'Of course, little goose. Where else do you think we go Crusading?'

'I . . . I just didn't think at all. The *Holy* Land . . . how wonderful! What was it like?'

'Hot.'

'And did you see Jerusalem? And was it really golden?'

Benedict coughed, and looked at Elvira warningly.

'No, it was rather dirty, as far as I remember,' said Sir Edward with a smile. 'Hot and dirty. Lots of fleas and camels, and lots of blood.'

'That's not how it is in the prayerbook,' thought Benedict. 'But I suppose a Crusader wouldn't know about *that.*'

As it happened, there *was* a flask of Jerusalem wine in the bag. Then followed a small silver crucifix, a dried herring, a red woollen cloak, and a great hunk of cheese, smelly and green with mould.

'No wonder the bag was so heavy,' laughed Sir Edward, weighing the green monstrosity in his hand, while the children held their noses. 'Shall we give this to the landlord tomorrow? He can make soup out of it.'

'For Master Shepherd,' said Benedict, and Elvira giggled delightedly.

'I'll see if there's anything left in the bag,' she said. 'I haven't found my sweets yet.'

'Ah, but the best always comes last,' said Sir Edward, smiling as Elvira's thin little arm vanished eagerly inside the depths of the bag.

Suddenly she looked puzzled.

'There's something *enormous* in here,' she squeaked. 'Something hard, and smooth, and knobbly. It's all knobbles. I wonder what it can be.'

'It sounds like a snake,' said Benedict solemnly, and Elvira made a face at him.

'It's heavy, whatever it is,' she said, tugging again at the mysterious object. 'It just won't move. I . . . ah, it's coming. It feels like a . . . But it *can't* be!'

'It can't be *what*?' said Sir Edward. 'Hurry up, poppet – don't keep us in suspense.'

There was a strange look on Elvira's face. She placed both hands in the bag, heaved hard, and then lifted out the mysterious object very slowly.

It was a Menorah. A great golden Menorah, studded with jewels and glittering like the sun.

And now a great silence came into the room. Elvira placed the Menorah on the floor, and both children crouched down and stared at it. But neither said a word.

'Over-awed,' thought Sir Edward. 'Their master shoemaker never had anything like *this* in his house. Strange . . . I'd forgotten I had it . . .' And suddenly he blushed and felt uncomfortable, remembering the night he had taken it from the burning synagogue in Maxenburg, hearing the hoof-beats in the silent street, and seeing again the murdered Jews lying across the threshold of the Ark they had tried to defend.

'I'd never looted before,' he thought. 'And I haven't looted since. I wish I didn't feel so guilty. *Everyone* loots, after all.'

And aloud he said cheerfully, 'Beautiful, isn't it? I dare say you never saw one of *these* before!'

Benedict tore his eyes away from the Menorah at last.

'Where did you get this?' he asked. His voice was accusing, but Sir Edward did not seem to notice this. It only occurred to him that the children were looking very pale. 'It's time they were in bed,' he thought. 'We've an early start tomorrow morning.'

He picked up the Menorah, and stroked its intricately carved branches. Crouched on the floor, the children still stared up at him.

'I got it from a Jewish synagogue,' he said. 'In a place called Maxenburg, a little town in Germany. We passed through there on our way home from the Crusades.'

'D-did they give it to you?' faltered Elvira, hoping against hope that her beloved Sir Edward had come by the Menorah honestly.

'Did *who* give it to me?'

'The J-Jews.'

The Crusader flung back his head and laughed.

'No, poppet, I took it,' he replied. 'After all, it didn't seem to belong to anybody any more.'

'W-why not?'

'Well, they were all dead. The Jews, I mean. And the synagogue was in ruins. So I decided to take this as a souvenir.'

Benedict swallowed hard.

'Who killed the Jews?' he asked grimly.

'Some of my men, I suppose,' replied Sir Edward casually, and he twisted the Menorah round in his hands so that the six-pointed star flashed like a jewel. 'I don't really know; *I* didn't join in. I don't care much for that sort of thing.'

'But you let your men do it?'

By now Sir Edward was beginning to find the cross-examination a little irritating. He smiled patiently at the children, and shook his head.

'It's bed now for you two,' he said firmly. 'And let's change the subject, shall we? Massacres and lootings, you don't want to talk about that sort of thing.'

'It's not the first time we've talked about it . . .' began Benedict. Then he saw Elvira looking at him with fearful eyes, and he stopped, afraid that he may have gone too far.

Sir Edward patted his head.

'Don't worry yourself about such things, my boy,' he said kindly. 'You're too sensitive. I don't like killing either . . . Don't tell anyone, but I don't even like hunting very much. These Jews though . . . I don't know much about them, but they're different. They're not like us. Everyone knows that. They're not the same as you and me.'

Benedict took a deep breath, and clenched his hands to keep them from trembling. The time had come, and there was nothing he could do about it.

He heard himself speak in a voice he did not even recognise as his own.

'We're Jews,' he said.

CHAPTER 9

The Knock

on the Door

THE rushlight was beginning to flicker; soon it would go out, thought Elvira, and the room would be plunged in darkness. She was almost sure she could hear the pounding of a drum somewhere in the night. It was some moments before she realised that the sound was the beating of her own heart.

Benedict heard nothing. He was aware only of Sir Edward's pale, shocked face. The Crusader had flopped down on the bed, and now he sat there, looking bewildered. On the floor the Menorah still blazed in its own pool of golden light.

'What will he do now?' thought Benedict tensely, and he waited, expecting Sir Edward's hand to reach for his dagger. But nothing happened.

'I wonder,' thought Benedict. 'I wonder what would happen if we made a run for it . . . Elvira and me . . . Would he go after us?'

Sir Edward looked back at Benedict gravely. And then, suddenly, he smiled.

'So *that's* why you wouldn't eat any meat!' he said. 'All that nonsense about having a fever years ago . . .

83

I *thought* it was a bit far-fetched.'

At first, Benedict was too taken aback to answer. Then he drew himself up to his full height.

'If you want us to go,' he said coldly, 'we'll go at once. Come along, Elvira.'

Sir Edward watched as the two children went towards the door. Then he sprang up, his face anxious. 'You're not going to desert me, are you?' he said, and there was a pleading note in his voice.

Benedict and Elvira gazed at him in astonishment. 'Not if you don't want us to,' faltered Benedict. 'B-but we thought . . .'

Sir Edward picked up the Menorah, and gently touched its branches.

'Come here and tell me what this is supposed to be,' he said. 'I suppose it *must* have some special meaning.'

His face was rather pink now, and he was fumbling awkwardly with the Menorah. Benedict looked at him in surprise, and then he understood. The great and terrifying Crusader, the man whose sword had struck terror into thousands of non-Christians, was as nervous as the children themselves.

A great feeling of relief flooded over Benedict. He had not felt so carefree since Robin Hood had discovered that he and Elvira were Jewish and had accepted them as friends just the same.

'It's a Chanukah candelabrum,' he explained. 'Chanukah is the Jewish feast of lights. You see, it commemorates the time when Judas Maccabeus defeated the Greeks and set us free from slavery . . .'

He began to tell the story in great detail, and Sir Edward sat patiently, trying to look intensely interested and not succeeding very well. But when Elvira joined in and began to describe the Chanukah parties they had had at home, his face became more alive, and his eyes sparkled.

'Do you remember the time Grandmother's honey-cake was so hard that Uncle Hugo had to cut it with his dagger?' said Elvira.

'Of course,' laughed Benedict. 'A great chunk of it jumped up in the air and hit him in the eye, remember?'

'And do you remember the time he set fire to his beard while he was lighting the candles, and Father threw wine in his face to put out the flames?'

'Your Uncle Hugo sounds a most unfortunate fellow,' commented Sir Edward.

'Oh, he is,' said Elvira cheerfully. 'Benedict, do you remember the time the dog chewed up his new shoes?'

And so it went on, Sir Edward listening with growing amusement and the children excitedly recalling all the Chanukah celebrations they had known. As they talked, the words tumbling over each other, it seemed to Sir Edward that he could see the red and gold study, the gold Menorah ablaze with fire, the happy family group laughing and singing and eating sweetmeats and playing games, and poor Uncle Hugo, his thin goat-like beard drenched in wine, hacking away furiously with his dagger at the honey-cake.

'Oh, didn't we have fun?' squealed Elvira, hopping up and down in her excitement. Then all at once the radiance died out of her face and she stood still, her head drooping.

'What's the matter?' said Sir Edward in surprise. 'Why this solemn face?'

'Because it's over now,' said Elvira sadly. 'They're all dead . . . Father, and Mother, and Grandmother, and Uncle Hugo, and everyone. Everyone except us.' And she sat down on the floor and began to cry.

Sir Edward suddenly felt very cold.

'A m-massacre, I suppose?' he said awkwardly.

Benedict nodded.

'In a place called Lymford,' he said quietly. 'It's a small town, a few miles from York.'

Sir Edward cleared his throat.

'I-I heard about the massacre at York,' he said. 'Three years ago, wasn't it? I didn't know about Lymford.'

'*Our* massacre was only a little one,' said Benedict bitterly. 'It wasn't very important. I don't suppose it will even be set down in the records.'

Sir Edward picked at the star on the Menorah as though he were trying to pick it to pieces.

'A ritual murder charge, was it?' he said at last.

'I beg your pardon?' said Benedict, puzzled.

'What was the reason? For the massacre, I mean.'

'Money,' replied Benedict. 'Baron Henry de Poulny owed the Jews money.'

And he began to tell the story of that last dreadful day in Lymford, Elvira chiming in every so often when his voice faltered.

It was the first time the children had allowed their minds to dwell on the massacre since Robin Hood had asked to know their story. During the last few days they had forced themselves to think of nothing but their mission, and London, and Oxford, and safety. But now, as they remembered, everything came back in a great rush of sound and colour, and they saw again the darkening square under the sunset sky, the yelling mob and the silent huddle of Jews, and they smelled smoke and heard the crackle and thunder of the flames that were devouring the Jewry.

Sir Edward, listening in silence, saw a very similar picture. Not in Lymford, but in the Jewries of Maxenburg and the other cities of Europe. There were his own soldiers, enlivening the boredom of the long journey to and from the Holy Land by killing a few

Jews and plundering a synagogue or two. And *he* sat playing chess in his great gilded tent, and the fleeing and wounded and dying Jews in the dark streets were no more flesh and blood than the jewelled knights and kings on his chess-board.

But now, somehow, the image was changed. In his mind every city had become Lymford, and every Jew had become a real person. Every hunted boy had Benedict's face, and every terrified little girl looked like Elvira.

The last words of Benedict's story died away. Sir Edward paced across the room and stood silent and shamefaced in the shadows.

'I wonder how you can ever trust a Christian again,' he said at last.

'There was Alaric,' replied Benedict. 'And Robin Hood. And the Outlaws.'

'And you,' Elvira added timidly, and she followed Sir Edward and slipped her hand into his. '*You've* never killed any Jews, have you? You said so.'

'Not with my own hands,' said Sir Edward gruffly. 'But I let it happen. I sat playing chess, and I didn't care. Well, how should I know that Jews were real people? I was always brought up to think of Jews as usurers. As the enemies of Christ. As the Devil. I don't think I've ever really had a conversation with a Jew till now.'

Benedict looked thoughtful.

'It's the same with us,' he said. 'Elvira, can you remember *us* ever having a real conversation with a Christian? In the old days, I mean?'

Elvira shook her head.

'We used to say good day,' she said. 'And talk about the weather, or the crops. But we never really *knew* any Christians. Not even Father's patients.'

Sir Edward smiled a little sadly.

'So, we've all three learned something,' he said. 'And now perhaps, in future, we'll remember. Whenever I see a group of Jews, I shall think "There may be a Benedict among these people. Or an Elvira. Or an Uncle Hugo" '.

'And when *we* see a group of Christians,' said Elvira, '*we'll* say "There may be a Sir Edward among them. Or a Robin Hood. Or a nice fat Friar Tuck" '.

'Isn't it strange?' The Crusader again fingered the star on the Menorah. 'Isn't it strange?' he mused. 'If anyone had told me a few weeks ago that I would be *sharing* danger with Jews today, I would never have believed them.'

It was the word 'danger' that made Benedict smile. 'But there *is* no danger now,' he thought. 'Now that Sir Edward knows everything, we're quite safe. He doesn't mind us being Jews. He still likes us.'

The feeling of relief was so enormous that Benedict felt quite lightheaded. All his tenseness was gone. He felt as though he could sink into the straw mattress and sleep for days and days.

It was at that moment that a thunderous knocking came on the attic door, and a gruff voice shouted 'Open, in the name of the Sheriff of Nottingham!'

Benedict thought at first that he must be dreaming. Then he saw the blood drain from Sir Edward's face, and heard Elvira begin to whimper in fear, and he knew that it was real enough.

'They've found us out,' he hissed. 'But *how?*'

'I suppose that fat pig recognised me after all.' muttered Sir Edward. 'But we can deny everything; it's only his word against ours.' And to Elvira he said 'Don't cry, sweetheart, or you'll give us all away.'

Elvira dried her eyes on her sleeve and tried to look calm. But just then the knocking came again – even louder, this time – and the gruff voice roared 'Are you going to open, or shall we break the door down?'

'Just a moment,' called Sir Edward. Then he quickly bundled the golden Menorah back into the saddlebag and pushed it under the mattress.

'We don't want our friend to see that,' he murmured. 'Now remember, children, I am William Holyard, no matter what Master Shepherd says. And try to look sleepy. We've been roused from our bed, remember?'

The children nodded, and looked at the door with frightened eyes.

Sir Edward pulled off his tunic, rumpled his hair, and then opened the door very slowly and yawned in the newcomer's face.

There were, in fact, *two* newcomers. One, the owner of the gruff, angry voice, was tall and fierce-looking; the other was chubby and looked more benevolent. Both wore stout leather tunics sewn with metal rings; they had metal helmets on their heads and carried lances, and manacles hung at their belts. It was obvious that they had come prepared for trouble.

'Master William Holyard?' said the fierce-looking man, glaring at Sir Edward.

Despite the frown, Sir Edward's first feeling was one of relief. The officer had called him 'William Holyard.' That must mean that his disguise had *not* been penetrated.

He bowed, and then stifled another yawn.

'To what do I owe the honour of this visit?' he asked.

The man scowled again.

'It's not a social call,' he snapped.

'I hardly thought it *was*,' replied Sir Edward lazily. 'It's rather late for social calls. We were all in bed when you knocked.'

'Yes, we're sleepy,' said Elvira indignantly, and Benedict silenced her with a warning 'ssssh!'

'If you want to know why we've come,' growled the man, 'we'll tell you. We've come about the horse.'

Sir Edward blinked in astonishment.

'*What* horse?' he asked.

'The horse you stole.'

'How dare you!' roared Sir Edward, now more angry than bewildered. 'I've never stolen any horses.'

'Well, Master Shepherd swears it's his,' the benevolent-looking man broke in. 'And he's a respected gentleman in these parts. *And* a friend of the Sheriff.'

'B-but I don't know what Master Shepherd is talking about,' protested Sir Edward. 'I've never touched his horse.'

'Master Shepherd saw it in the stable of this inn less than an hour ago, so you needn't deny it,' said the fierce man sternly. 'A handsome chestnut . . . the ostler told us your son was riding it when you arrived here this evening. Master Shepherd recognised it at once as a horse stolen from him in Sherwood Forest only last month. By Robin Hood.'

At the mention of Robin Hood's name, Sir Edward felt his heart sink.

'There . . . there must be some mistake,' he muttered, mopping his brow and feeling it damp with sweat.

'No mistake at all,' said the fierce man. 'The horse was branded on the fetlock with Master Shepherd's mark. Now, what we want to know is *how* you obtained this horse from Robin Hood. He's a friend of yours, I take it?'

'No.'

'Well, an acquaintance, then? You've met him?'

'If I *had* met him I'm sure I should remember,' stuttered Sir Edward, aware that both children were gazing at him imploringly. 'Don't look at me like that,' he thought. 'I can't work miracles.'

'We shall have to refresh your memory, I can see,' growled the fierce man, swinging his lance in a menacing fashion.

'I . . . I don't understand what this is all about,' said Sir Edward desperately.

'Perhaps the Sheriff himself will explain it more clearly,' the benevolent-looking man broke in. 'You'd better come with us to Nottingham, and be introduced to him. And if you *are* a friend of Robin Hood, then Heaven help you!'

He pointed his lance at Sir Edward's breast, his benevolent look quite gone now, and the other man came up behind the Crusader and began to manacle his arms behind his back. And then Benedict had a sudden flash of inspiration. The best idea, in fact, that he had ever had. It was so brilliant that he felt like shouting for joy.

He ran forward and flung himself at Sir Edward's feet.

'It was *my* fault, father,' he cried. '*I* stole the horse. At Nottingham Fair.'

'What?' gasped Sir Edward, thinking that the boy must have gone mad, while Elvira gaped at her brother in bewilderment.

'Don't you remember, sir?' said Benedict. 'You gave me money to buy a horse at Nottingham Fair. But I . . . I didn't buy one.' His head drooped in shame. 'I . . . I saw the chestnut tethered to a post, so I . . . I took it. And I spent the money you gave me on sweet-meats and amusements. I'm sorry, Father. I won't do it again.'

Sir Edward understood now. But the men-at-arms were so taken aback that the fierce one dropped his manacles with a clatter, letting the Crusader go free.

'Here's a fine story for a father to hear!' he gasped.

'So the boy's a thief, is he?'

Sir Edward, realising that it was up to him to play the horrified father, buried his face in his hands.

'A thief,' he murmured brokenly. 'My son a thief . . . Have I lived to see this day?'

The benevolent-looking man-at-arms threw back his head and roared with laughter.

'The young devil!' he chuckled. 'He's really turned the tables on Robin Hood, hasn't he? First Robin steals Master Shepherd's horse, and then this young scamp comes along and robs *him*. It's the best joke I've heard in weeks.'

'It's no joke for him,' said his friend sourly, cocking his thumb at Benedict. 'He won't feel so pleased with himself tomorrow, when he meets the Sheriff.'

Benedict's heart lurched. He looked up and saw that Sir Edward had turned quite pale.

'B-b-but if I recompense Master Shepherd for the horse . . .?' the Crusader began.

'Master Shepherd doesn't want money,' replied the fierce man-at-arms. 'He's got plenty of money of his own. He's very angry, and he wants vengeance.'

'I-I'll give him double the cost of the horse.'

'He won't take it. He's a righteous man, is Master Shepherd, and he believes that thieves ought to be punished.'

Sir Edward pressed Benedict's arm reassuringly. Then he turned back to the men-at-arms.

'I shall appeal to the Sheriff,' he said firmly. 'I shall explain that this was only a youthful escapade.'

'You can do that tomorrow, sir,' said the other man-at-arms. 'But, in the meantime, this young fellow must come with us to Nottingham.' And he picked up the manacles and began to chain Benedict's hands behind his back.

Sir Edward fumbled for his dagger. But Benedict

looked at him warningly, and his hand dropped to his side again.

'He's still a child, as you see,' he said. 'I'm sure your Sheriff will be merciful.'

'I shouldn't rely on that, sir,' the benevolent man-at-arms replied with a kindly smile. 'The last horse-thief we hanged was only twelve years old. And that was a week ago.'

CHAPTER 10

Benedict Grows Up

IT was the dull 'thump, thump' of a hammer on wood that woke Benedict, and for a few moments he lay with his eyes shut, wondering what it could be.

One of the Outlaws, he thought drowsily, must be felling a tree; the supply of brushwood had run out. Soon someone would light a fire, and the mingled early-morning smell of smoke and dewy grass and roasting venison and hot mulled wine would fill his nostrils. And then he would slowly open his eyes and see the bright blue morning sky glinting through the green thatch of the forest.

Benedict *did* open his eyes, and almost shut them again in terror. He was not in Sherwood at all; he was in a tiny, dark, stone-flagged room with a huge iron door. And the only glimpse of sky he could see came to him through a small window striped with heavy iron bars.

His whole body felt stiff and bruised. Groaning with pain, Benedict struggled into a sitting position. And as he did so, everything that had happened the previous night came back to him. His arrest by the Sheriff's men; a recollection of being chained, and dragged down the staircase of the inn; Elvira's pale, frightened face peering between the railings; Henry Shepherd laughing and slapping one of the men-at-arms on the back, and the other guests, dripping tankards in their hands, standing and staring. And then one of the men-at-arms had slung him across a horse, and Sir Edward had insisted on accompanying him and appealing to the Sheriff, and then they had all gone galloping off through the night, with Benedict jolting up and down so hard that he was nearly sick. And finally they had brought him to a great, gaunt, frowning castle . . . he had seen it illuminated by flares and torches against the black, night sky . . . and torn him away from Sir Edward, and hustled him up many narrow, winding steps to this cell, and thrown him down on a heap of straw and old rags, and then locked him in and left him.

And now it was morning. Soon, perhaps, he would know what they meant to do with him. One of the men-at-arms had said something about hanging. But surely that must have been a joke?

Benedict felt a nasty, cold sensation creep through his stomach. Last night he had been brave; he had even managed to whisper to Sir Edward that he and Elvira must set off for London at once, early in the morning, before the Sheriff could begin to make enquries. 'I shall be all right, sir,' he had said. 'Don't worry about me.' But now, alone, he realised that he was frightened, a small boy at the mercy of strong, bad men.

Suddenly he heard a clinking noise, and then the rusty sound of a key turning in the lock, and he held his breath and waited.

Very, very slowly the door crept open, and a face

peered cautiously round the edge. It was a stupid face, with its round, pale eyes and open mouth, but it did not look cruel. Benedict recognised it as belonging to the jailer he had seen the night before.

This morning the jailer was smiling in quite a friendly way, much to Benedict's relief. He was carrying a plate and a small, earthenware jug, and this cheered Benedict even more. At least, he thought, they did not intend to starve him to death.

' 'Morning', said the jailer brightly. 'Breakfast.' He placed the plate and jug on the floor, and then locked the door very slowly and carefully.

Breakfast consisted of water and a large piece of rather stale black bread. Benedict began to eat the bread hungrily, and the jailer lolled against the wall and watched him benevolently.

'Nice morning,' he commented, when Benedict had finished. 'Just the weather for a nice long walk,' he added, rather tactlessly. But Benedict did not mind; *he* was thinking that it was just the morning for a nice long ride. He hoped that Sir Edward and Elvira had got off to an early start, before Henry Shepherd had begun to entertain any new suspicions. In his mind's eye he saw the sunlight glittering on the hills, and the two riders cantering along the road to London. By now, very likely, they would have left Nottingham far behind.

And at that thought, Benedict suddenly felt very lonely and frightened again.

'W-what are they going to do to me?' he asked, and he could not stop his voice from trembling.

'Oh, don't worry – you'll have a trial,' said the jailer amiably. 'Our prisoners all get trials. Fair trials. And then—' He wet his finger, and drew it meaningly across his throat.

'I don't believe it; they're only trying to frighten

me,' thought Benedict desperately. He was about to ask some more questions. How long it would be before he was tried, perhaps. But the jailer suddenly gathered up the empty plate and jug, and began to unlock the door. 'Can't stand gossiping here all day,' he said. And then he was gone, and Benedict was left alone.

He stood on tiptoe by the window and tried to peer out, but all he could see was sky, and the tail-end of the long road as it vanished into the distant hills. The hammering noise had stopped. Just a workman, he thought, busy with some repairs in the castle keep.

And now the silence was broken by the sound of hoofs clattering into the courtyard, and the jingle of harness as the rider dismounted.

Was it the Sheriff? wondered Benedict. Or one of his men? Or was it just someone coming to visit a prisoner? In a few moments the courtyard was still again. Idly, the boy shifted from one foot to another, wondering how he was going to pass the time. If only he had something to read . . . Father had always taught him that time not spent with his books was time wasted. Father had been the finest scholar of all the Jews in Lymford, and now he was dead. Benedict himself had spent most of the long hours of his childhood in study, and soon he, too, would die. What use was learning, after all?

A key grated in the lock, and the door again slowly opened to reveal his jailer's stupid, amiable face.

'Nice morning,' he commented, after a short pause.

'Is *that* all you've come here to tell me?' thought Benedict irritably. But aloud he said 'Is it?'

'Yes,' replied the jailer. 'And I've got something for you. Something you'll like.'

For a moment, Benedict hoped that the 'something' might be a book, or another meal. But the jailer was empty-handed.

'It's a visitor,' he said at last. 'Your father. He's come to see you.'

Benedict was shocked. So shocked, in fact, that his knees buckled, and he had to sit down on the bed. He had been consoling himself with the thought that Sir Edward and Elvira were out of harm's way. And now Sir Edward was here, in Nottingham Castle, under the very eyes of his enemies. And Elvira, where was *she*?

For a moment, Benedict thought of refusing to see his 'father'. If he did that, he reasoned, Sir Edward would leave the Castle and be safe. But as he opened his mouth to protest he saw that it was already too late. Sir Edward had followed the jailer, and was now standing in the doorway of the cell.

The Crusader, Benedict noticed, was looking very pale and tired. His cloak was dusty and his hair tousled under his velvet cap. Obviously he had been riding long and hard, but where? And *what* had he done with Elvira?

For a few moments Benedict and Sir Edward stood staring at each other, and neither said a word. But the jailer saw nothing strange in their silence. 'There he is, Master Holyard,' he said kindly. 'Well and happy, as you see.' And Benedict thought it as well to follow his up with a polite 'Good day, Father.'

Sir Edward took a step forward, and then stopped and turned towards the jailer.

'May I have a few minutes *alone* with my son?' he said pointedly.

The jailer seemed about to protest, but Sir Edward thrust his hand into his pouch and brought out a shining coin. Without a word the jailer pocketed it, smiled, nodded, and then sidled out of the cell and locked the door behind him, leaving Benedict and Sir Edward alone together.

Benedict was now surprised to find that he was glad to see Sir Edward after all. He felt a sudden impulse to throw his arms round the Crusader, and cling to him, and bury his head in the dusty cloak.

But he stopped short when he saw the expression on his face. For Sir Edward, it was plain, was very angry.

'That was a stupid thing you did, wasn't it?' he said at last.

Benedict was taken aback.

'I don't think it was stupid,' he said sulkily. 'It worked, didn't it?'

'Not for you.' Sir Edward came forward and gripped Benedict's arm. 'Don't you realise,' he said, 'that they might hang you, and that I couldn't do a thing to stop it?' And Benedict, to his own surprise, found himself replying 'I don't want you to do anything. I only want you to escape. With Elvira. W-where *is* she?'

'Elvira is safe. With Robin Hood. I rode back to Sherwood Forest last night, after I had spoken to the Sheriff, and left her there.'

'So Robin knows about last night . . . What did he say?' asked Benedict, too relieved to know that Elvira was in good hands to care very much about the answer.

'Robin agrees with me that you were very rash,' said Sir Edward grimly. 'If only you had kept quiet, we might have bluffed our way out of it somehow. I might have thought of something. But now . . . I've already told the Sheriff that I would be glad to recompense Henry Shepherd for his horse, but it seems Shepherd won't hear of it. All he wants is revenge. So now there's only one thing left for me to do. I shall have to go back to the Sheriff, and tell him the truth.'

'No, you mustn't!' cried Benedict, and he clutched desperately at Sir Edward's sleeve. 'If you do that, you'll *never* reach London. The Sheriff is in league with Prince John; I've heard Robin say so. He'd do anything to stop the ransom from getting to King Richard. He'll have you killed if he finds out who you are. No, you must never tell him!'

'But, you silly child,' said Sir Edward, greatly surprised at this outburst, 'I can't let you take the blame for my actions. What kind of knight would I be if I let you suffer? The mission is mine, after all, and the dangers must also be mine.'

'The mission is mine too,' cried Benedict vehemently, and Sir Edward looked at him in astonishment.

'I don't understand,' he said at last. 'It's not even as though you were a true Englishman.'

'Maybe not. But I'm a true Jew.'

'I don't doubt it. But what has that got to do with King Richard's ransom?'

Benedict walked to the window, and looked out. There was not a cloud in the sky; its soft, blue expanse seemed to hold the promise of summer, of a happier future, of peaceful times for the Jews of England.

'Listen,' he said, turning back to Sir Edward. 'This probably hasn't occurred to you, But Robin understood. As long as King Richard is away, the Jews in this country will be in danger. Massacres everywhere . . . in big places like York . . . in little places like Lymford . . . Maybe even in Oxford. If the King were at home, our enemies wouldn't dare. The Jews belong to the King.'

Sir Edward's jaw dropped.

'Then is *that* why . . . ?' he began.

'Yes. That was why we agreed to go with you. And that's why *you* must escape. Even if I . . . if I don't.'

'And you would really be prepared to die for people you don't even know?'

Benedict smiled.

'But Jews have been dying for the Jewish people ever since the world began,' he said gently. 'My father told me that...'

And as he said this Benedict saw again, in memory, Father's study on a warm, summer morning three years ago. Himself crouched, reluctantly, over his books, wishing he could be out in the sunshine. And Uncle Hugo bursting in, pale and wild-eyed, to tell Father the terrible news that had just come from York.

For some time after being told how the Jews of York had locked themselves in Clifford's Tower and died there, amid the smoke and flames and the joyful shouts of the mob, Father had sat hunched in his chair, his face ashen, hearing neither Uncle Hugo's noisy laments nor the insistent cry of the blackbird on the lawn outside the study window.

Then, suddenly, he had turned to Benedict and said, very calmly, 'My son, even this senseless murder has its purpose. Judaism becomes a little stronger each time Jews are prepared to die for it. Remember, if ever *we* should be called on to die for our faith, that we shall be building a highway for those who come after us.'

Father's words had made little impression on Benedict then. For the children of Lymford the massacre at York had meant only a holiday, a brief respite from lessons, while their elders had crowded into the synagogue to weep and pray. But now, as he stood facing Sir Edward in the cell at Nottingham Castle, he at last understood what Father had been trying to tell him. All at once he felt that he was himself part of a chain that stretched far back into the past, linking him with all the martyrs and heroes. And he saw the highway along which the Jews would walk in the future, proud and unafraid.

Suddenly he was filled with a kind of exultation.
'I'm not frightened any more,' he whispered to himself. And for a little while it was true.

Sir Edward still looked unconvinced.

'I can understand why grown men should want to
die for their faith,' he said. 'But you're a child.'

Benedict proudly pulled himself up to his full height.
'In four weeks' time I shall be Barmitzvah,' he said
proudly. 'That means that I shall celebrate my
thirteenth birthday, and be confirmed. And at thirteen
a Jewish boy becomes a man.'

The knight patted his shoulder awkwardly.

'You're a man already,' he said in a gruff voice.
'And a better man than most.'

'Then will you promise . . . ?'

'I'll keep faith with you, never fear.'

Sir Edward might have said more, but at that
moment the jailer put his face round the door to
announce, very regretfully, that the private interview
was over.

'After all, you might be plotting how to escape,'
he said. 'And where would my job be then?'

Sir Edward relieved his feelings by aiming a vicious
kick at Benedict's bed.

'I don't think much of this cell!' he roared. 'Just
look at that pile of old rags. It's disgusting.'

The jailer looked a little hurt.

'We do our best, sir,' he muttered. 'At least we don't
have rats, like some do. Or fleas. This is a very clean
prison sir.'

Sir Edward turned again to pat Benedict's shoulder.

'Don't worry any more, my boy,' he said in a hearty
voice. 'We'll think of some way to get you released,
never fear. Just leave it all to me.'

After Sir Edward had gone Benedict stood on

tiptoe at the window, hoping to catch a last glimpse of him. But he could see nothing; his cell was too far from the ground. He could only hear the jingle of harness, and then the clatter of hoofs as the Crusader rode out of the castle courtyard.

A few minutes later the jailer was back, his pouch bulging with fruit, which he tossed to Benedict.

'A very nice gentleman, your father,' he commented. 'Give me a gold piece.'

'So I'm going to be a privileged prisoner . . . for the next few days, at least,' thought Benedict, and he picked up a handful of cherries and began to nibble them with relish.

He was suddenly aware that the hammering noise which had woken him that morning had started again. The jailer also noticed it, and cocked an ear towards the window.

'Ah, they're at it again,' he said cheerfully. 'Been having breakfast, the workmen have. Pork pasty and ale. Now they're back on the job.'

'What are they doing, then?' said Benedict idly, his mouth full of cherries.

'Hammering.'

'Yes, I know. But *what* are they hammering?'

'They're building a new gallows. The old one got burnt down last week. And *that* was no accident, if you ask me. They're working full speed on this one. Seems like they'll be needing it soon.'

Benedict felt as though his cherries were choking him. All his new courage seemed to ooze away. Desperately he ran to the window. and clung to the bars. For one moment, far away on the distant ribbon of highway, he caught a glimpse of Sir Edward spurring his horse towards the hills. His bridle flashed as it caught the sun, and then he was gone.

CHAPTER 11

The Rescue

THREE days later, two very strange visitors called at Nottingham Castle and asked to see Benedict.

One was a stout, pompous-looking priest wearing a hat several sizes too big for him. The other was a gawky, bewildered-looking boy whose thin arms sagged under the weight of an enormous book. His clothes seemed to hang on him; his hat came down so low that it practically rested on his nose, and he walked as though his feet hurt. The sentry on guard blinked and rubbed his eyes as this peculiar-looking pair shuffled across the drawbridge and came to an obedient halt at the gate.

'God be with you, my son,' said the priest in a falsetto voice so high that it was almost a squeak. 'I am Father Angelicus, of the Church of St Peter-in-the-Mire. I have come to give what spiritual consolation I can to the boy John Holyard. I believe he has been charged with stealing a horse?'

'Yes, Father.'

'Sad, very sad. I hate to see mere children falling into sin and depravity.' And the priest looked very doleful, and wiped his eyes on the sleeve of his robe.

'And this?' said the sentry, looking down with some surprise at the forlorn-looking boy, who was clinging desperately to the big book and trying hard to keep his hat on at the same time.

'This is my servant . . . and between you and me, he's not worth his keep. If you drop that book I'll drop *you* in the moat, you scoundrel!' And the priest sized the boy by the neck of his baggy tunic, and shook him soundly.

The sentry tried hard not to laugh.

'I hope you will bring the young thief to true repentance, Father,' he said gravely, and he stood aside politely from the gate so that the odd-looking couple could pass through.

Benedict was lying on his heap of straw, staring up listlessly at the ceiling of his cell, when his jailer came in to announce that he had visitors.

In fact there had been no visitors at all since Sir Edward had come and gone three days earlier. Apart from his jailer the boy had seen no one. Not even the Sheriff, or Henry Shepherd. Time had gone by slowly and heavily, seventy-two dragging hours each made up of sixty leaden minutes, with no one to talk to but his jailer (who was not a brilliant conversationalist), and nothing to do but think.

Even the workmen in the courtyard had packed up their tools and gone. The gallows, thought Benedict, must be completed by now. In his mind's eye he saw it, the bright new cross-beams shining in the sunlight; the noose swinging idly in the soft air. He shuddered, and tried to shut out the image, but it persisted.

'They *can't* hang me,' he said to himself a dozen times a day. But in his heart he knew that they could, and he felt helpless and abandoned.

And so he was not in the best of moods when his jailer told him that Father Angelicus had come to give him spiritual consolation.

'I'm a Jew; what do *I* want with a Christian clergyman?' he thought angrily. But aloud, all he said was 'I won't see him.'

The jailer looked shocked.

'But he's come to pray with you,' he said. 'It's very good of him to bother.'

'I don't want to pray with anyone.'

'But he's had all these stairs to climb,' the jailer persisted. 'And he's a stout gentleman, with all due respect. At least you can let him come in and sit down for a few minutes.'

Benedict felt he he could not very well refuse this request. So he nodded sulkily, and then went and stood by the window with his back turned resolutely towards the door.

A few moments later he heard the door swing open with a screech of hinges. A high-pitched voice said 'Bless you, my son,' and the jailer gave a pleased chuckle and replied 'I'll leave you alone with him for a few minutes, your worship.' Then the door clanged shut again, and Benedict heard the high-pitched voice declare 'So this is the young horse-thief. Sad, very sad.'

Benedict swung round to face the priest – and then blinked in astonishment, just as the sentry had done. Father Angelicus, his eyes almost hidden by the huge hat, was certainly an odd-looking figure, and the servant boy, who must have been about Benedict's age, looked even odder. He seemed to be falling out of his clothes, and all that could be seen of his face, under the hat, was a mouth that seemed on the verge of saying something.

Benedict rubbed his eyes. Not simply because priest

and boy looked so peculiar, but because there was
something vaguely familiar about both of them.

'There *can't* be,' he thought. 'I've never seen them
before in my life.'

Father Angelicus gripped the servant boy by the
ear, and dragged him forward.

'There you are,' he said in his high falsetto voice.
'There's the young thief. Take a good look at him.
You'll end up in a prison cell if you're not more
careful, mark my words. God knows how many sweetmeats you've stolen out of my pantry! Let this be a
lesson to you.'

The servant boy was obviously impressed. So
impressed, in fact, that he dropped the huge book,
which fell with a crash on the priest's toe.

'Idiot!' shrilled Father Angelicus, aiming a blow at
the boy's head, and missing. 'You'd drop your own
hands if they weren't joined on!'

Benedict had watched this scene with some enjoy-
ment. It made a welcome change, he thought, from
the dull routine of prison life. But when Father
Angelicus finally opened his book and said 'Come
now, young sinner, will you join me in a prayer?', he
turned aside and walked again towards the window.

For a few moments he stood silent, peering out
through the bars, while the intonation of a Latin
prayer filled the cell. Then, suddenly, a defiant mood
came upon him. He felt he did not care, now, what
happened to him. Clutching the bars till his knuckles
were quite white, he cried out 'Shema Yisroel! Hear,
O Israel, the Lord our God, the Lord is one!'

What happened next was very surprising.

The priest stopped chanting. But instead of showing
anger, or surprise, he merely chuckled.

'You haven't changed, have you, Benedict?' he said,
his shrill falsetto changed suddenly to a deep, familiar

boom. 'Still the same pig-headed young idiot. Quite resigned to being hanged, are you?'

'Friar Tuck!' cried Benedict, his own voice shrill with disbelief. 'It . . . it *is* you, isn't it? But . . . but . . . *how*?'

'Robin sent me, of course.' And Friar Tuck pulled off his hat, revealing the rosy jovial face that Benedict had last seen among the green arbours of Sherwood.

'Friar Tuck! I . . . I can't believe it,' cried Benedict, and he hurled himself into the friar's stout arms and received a hug that nearly cracked his ribs.

'Well, how are you?' boomed Friar Tuck, and he looked down into the boy's wan face and shook his head sadly. 'Are you getting enough to eat? You look skinnier than ever.'

'I'm all right.'

'You don't look all right. Robin would be very angry if he could see you now. And that reminds me . . . Robin has sent me here with a most ingenious escape device. Very clever. I wish I'd thought of it.'

'D-do you mean,' faltered Benedict, 'that you've come here to help me escape?'

'Well, I certainly didn't come all this way just to pray at you.'

All at once Benedict felt as though he were climbing out of a dark pit into the sunlight.

'Escape,' he thought. 'Not to die, after all . . .'

Through a kind of haze he realised that Friar Tuck was still speaking.

'Now, let me explain all the details of this plan,' he was saying. 'But, first of all, I must introduce you to my accomplice.' And he nodded towards the gawky servant-boy, who was still gazing at Benedict open-mouthed.

Benedict looked curiously at what could be seen of the boy's face, and again felt that strange sense of familiarity.

'Don't you recognise him?' chuckled Friar Tuck. Then, with a sudden motion, he whisked off the boy's huge hat, and a mane of long, black hair tumbled about a face that was no longer that of a stranger.

'Elvira!' gasped Benedict, and the little girl smiled shyly.

'Do I look funny?' she asked, looking down at her baggy tunic and breeches with some embarrassment.

'You do, a little,' said Benedict. 'But it's good to see you,' he added tactfully.

'The sentry at the gate thought I was a boy,' Elvira added proudly. 'So I suppose I must look like one.'

Benedict smiled back at Elvira, and then felt vaguely puzzled – he did not quite know why. She *was* Elvira, now that the engulfing hat was gone . . . and yet somehow she was different. He hugged her, and then all at once he knew what had been puzzling him.

'You've grown taller,' he cried. 'You never used to be as tall as me!'

Friar Tuck chuckled.

'We *made* her taller,' he said. 'Robin Hood doesn't let a little thing like that stand in his way. It's all part of the escape plot. Show him your feet sweetheart.'

Elvira lifted her foot, and Benedict understood why she had been walking so gingerly. Lashed to the soles of her shoes with string were additional soles made of wood. They were at least three inches thick.

'You can take these off now,' said Friar Tuck cheerfully, and he wrenched off the wooden soles and pushed them under the heap of straw.

The boy watched, fascinated, as Elvira shrank to her original size again. Then he turned towards Friar Tuck.

'Excuse me, sir, but what *is* the escape plot?' he asked.

'Didn't I tell you? Very remiss of me. It's a very good idea. I wish I'd thought of it.'

'Yes, sir,' replied Benedict patiently.

'Now, listen carefully,' boomed the Friar. 'I don't want to have to repeat all this again. Now, your sister, under this oversized outfit – it's deliberately oversized, my boy, it's meant to fit *you* – is wearing her own pretty dress. What *you* are going to do is to put on her tunic and breeches, *and* the hat . . . the hat is very important . . . and walk out of this castle with me, as my servant. Carrying my book. All very simple, eh?'

'Yes,' said Benedict, wondering whether he had heard right. 'B-b-but . . .'

'Now, you haven't found any snags, have you?' said Friar Tuck reproachfully.

'Y-yes, sir. I'm afraid so.'

'I knew it. I felt it in my bones,' boomed the Friar. 'You always were an argumentative type, young Benedict. Come along, what is it?'

'How is Elvira going to get out?'

'She'll *walk* out, of course. With us,' said Friar Tuck, his eyebrows raised in surprise.

'What as?'

'As herself, of course.'

'B-b-but what is the jailer going to say?' stuttered Benedict, thinking that either he or Friar Tuck must have gone mad. 'He knows that no little girl came in with you.'

Elvira looked frightened. But the Friar merely chuckled.

'I don't know that he'll remember anything of the kind,' he said. 'Haven't you noticed yet that the man is a complete fool? If he wasn't the Sheriff's wife's cousin he would have been thrown out long ago.'

'B-b-but . . .'

'Don't fritter away our precious time in pointless arguments, boy. Well, what is it now?'

'He'll find *m-me* gone . . .'

'No he won't. We've thought of that too. We're going to make an effigy of you, and leave it in your bed.'

'An effigy?' faltered Benedict, thinking of the dead knights and ladies who, Father had once told him, lay sound asleep in grey marble in the church at Lymford.

'Oh, nothing elaborate,' replied the Friar. 'We'll just stuff a few rags inside the clothes you take off when you put on Elvira's clothes. I'll tell the jailer you've fallen asleep. He won't notice the difference till he goes to wake you. Long after we've gone, I hope.'

Benedict said nothing more. But all the time he was exchanging his clothes for the tunic and breeches Elvira had been wearing, his anxiety grew and grew.

'But supposing the jailer *does* remember that you didn't have a little girl with you?' he said at last.

Friar Tuck put down the 'effigy' he was making, and looked exasperated.

'It isn't good for a young fellow like you to have such a worrying nature,' he said at last. 'When *I* was your age, I was as carefree as a bird.'

'Yes, but . . .'

'If he *does* notice, we'll just have to do something to keep him quiet.'

'We're not going to *kill* him, are we?' squealed Elvira, aghast.

'Kill him?' It was Friar Tuck's turn to look aghast now. 'Of course we won't kill him. We'll tie him up, that's all. With your girdle. Yes, that's a good idea, isn't it? Here, I'd better have it, just in case.' And Friar Tuck, looking pleased with himself, drew out his clasp-knife and neatly hacked a length off Elvira's girdle, which was made of linen delicately embroidered with crimson rosebuds.

Elvira looked so horrified that Benedict forgot his anxiety and nearly laughed aloud. But Friar Tuck was not looking at Elvira. Still beaming, he carefully divided the embroidered strip into two equal lengths.

'One for his wrists and one for his ankles,' he explained. 'Lucky dog . . . I'll wager he's never been tied up with rosebuds before.'

Benedict looked worried again.

'B-but what will happen to him?' he faltered. 'After we've gone, I mean? I don't want him to starve to death up here. It wouldn't be fair.'

Friar Tuck laughed, and patted his head.

'You're a good lad,' he said. 'No harm will come to your jailer, I promise. The other jailers will notice his absence when he doesn't come to supper, and they'll search for him. And, by the time they find him, *we'll* be far away . . .'

Reassured on this point, Benedict turned to look critically at Friar Tuck's 'effigy.'

'It doesn't look like me,' he said at last.

'Oh, it *does*,' squealed Elvira delightedly, and was rewarded with a pinch.

'It's got one leg fatter than the other,' Benedict went on.

Friar Tuck grunted.

'Don't be so *fussy*, boy,' he boomed. 'I'm a friar – not a master sculptor. He'll do.' And he patted the scarecrow-like figure lovingly, and then arranged it on the heap of straw and carefully piled the rest of the rags over it.

'Sound asleep,' he grinned. 'Mind you don't wake him. Benedict, you'd better put your hat on. Our friend the jailer will soon be coming back to see what headway we've made with our prayers.'

When the jailer *did* at last return, both children found themselves watching his stupid, amiable face anxiously. Was he as stupid as all *that*? Would he notice Elvira? Would he raise the alarm before he could be silenced?

Benedict held his breath as the jailer's pale blue eyes roamed idly round the cell.

'Where's the prisoner gone, then?' he said at last.

'Oh, *that's* all right,' Friar Tuck assured him calmly. 'He's asleep. Worn out with penitence and emotion, poor young sinner.' And he nodded sadly in the direction of the crumpled figure lying so still under the heap of rags.

But the jailer did not even glance at the 'effigy'. His eyes had come to rest on Elvira, and his face puckered in surprise.

'Where did *she* come from?' he said at last.

Elvira clutched nervously at Benedict's sleeve. But Friar Tuck smiled at the jailer, apparently unperturbed.

'Why, my good man, she came in with me,' he boomed.

'No she didn't. There was only you and the lad.'

'You've got rather a poor memory, haven't you, my son?' said Friar Tuck kindly.

'No, I ain't. I can remember lots of things, your honour. And what I say is that there's something funny going on here.'

Friar Tuck sighed.

'You're right, of course, my son,' he said after a pause. 'I should have known better than to try to fool *you*. You're entitled to an explanation, and you shall have it. Now, before I tell you where the little girl came from, there are one or two things you ought to know. To start with, would you oblige me by looking out of the window and telling me what you see?'

His face alight with curiosity, the jailer crossed to the window and peered out through the bars. He did not feel the Friar slip Elvira's girdle round his ankles until the linen strip tightened, and then he looked back from the window in angry bewilderment. 'There's nothing down there that *I* can see . . .' he began. 'Here, what's going on? Why've you tied my feet up? Stop it, you young gallows-birds . . .' For the children had slipped behind him and were clutching desperately at his arms.

Before he could quite realise what was happening, the jailer's wrists had been pinioned behind his back with the other strip of girdle.

'We don't bear you any ill-will,' said Friar Tuck soothingly, 'but I'm afraid we can't tell you anything more. We shall have to gag you as well. But don't worry . . . it won't hurt.' Before the jailer could open his mouth to protest the Friar had wrapped a strip of rag round it, and the words came out as an angry gurgle.

Friar Tuck turned to beam at the children.

'There, that wasn't difficult, was it?' he said. 'We'll prop our friend up in the corner – he'll be more comfortable there – and then we'll be off.'

Trying to ignore the jailer's furiously rolling eyes and the indignant grunts that were coming from behind the gag, Benedict helped Friar Tuck settle him as comfortably as possible in a corner of the cell. Then the Friar bent and patted the man's head.

'You'll soon be rescued, my son,' he said. 'I'll wager you won't even miss your supper. Herring pasty on Thursdays, isn't it? Remember to have a second helping; you deserve it. Come, children . . . we don't want to stay in this gloomy place longer than we need, do we?'

As he clambered carefully down the dank, dark

spiral staircase that led from the cells to the castle courtyard, Benedict held his breath. He could not believe that he was so nearly free. There was still the sentry at the gate to be faced, but surely he would not remember Father Angelicus and his retinue. So many people came and went all day. No, *he* would certainly have forgotten.

The steps were steep and coated with slime, and the stone walls smelt of long years of imprisonment. Benedict kept his eyes on Friar Tuck's broad, serge-clad back. In a few moments, he told himself, he would be out in the sunlight, and it would caress him more gently than it had ever done in all his life.

And now the great iron-studded door swung open, and Benedict was engulfed in a flood of light so brilliant that it made him blink. Ahead lay the moat and the gateway, and beyond that stretched the meadows and the distant hills, glowing emerald and amethyst and amber and so close that he felt he could reach out and touch them.

'Free,' he murmured, and Friar Tuck's large, chubby hand clasped his own encouragingly.

'A few moments more,' whispered the friar. 'Come, children.' And he strode fearlessly up to the sentry at the gate and greeted him with a cheerful 'God be with you, my son.'

'And with you, Father,' replied the sentry. He glanced idly at Benedict, and the boy felt his tense body relax. Then he stiffened again as he saw the sentry's eyes move enquiringly to Elvira.

Friar Tuck also noticed the surprised look on the sentry's face, and he tried to slip quickly through the gateway. But an outstretched lance held him back.

'Just a moment, Father,' said the sentry politely. 'Where did this little girl come from?'

'W-where did she come from?' faltered Friar Tuck,

feeling the children press against him in terror. 'She
. . . she . . . why, she came with *me*, of course. She's
one of my parishioners.'

'But I didn't see her go *in* with you. You had this
lad here, but no girl. I would have remembered a
little girl,' persisted the sentry.

A wave of misery swept over Benedict. 'To be sent
back to that cell,' he thought, 'after smelling the
summer air once again. No, I simply couldn't bear
it . . .'

Friar Tuck, meanwhile, was thinking desperately.
The sentry was eyeing him, waiting for an explanation . . . and he knew it would have to be a good one.

'I wish Robin Hood was here,' he thought. '*He*
has all the brilliant ideas.' And then a brilliant idea
of his own came to him.

He placed his hand confidingly on the sentry's
shoulder, and dropped his voice.

'The truth is,' he said, 'that the child's mother has
been having some trouble with her. Stealing. Cakes
and preserves, you know, from the pantry. So the
mother asked me . . . begged me with tears in her
eyes, poor, honest woman . . . to take her to see the
little boy who is in prison. To teach her a lesson. To
show her what happens to children who steal. I'm
glad to say she was suitably impressed.'

The sentry looked rather less impressed.

'I'm happy to hear that she has learned her lesson,
Father,' he replied. 'But all this doesn't explain why
I didn't see her go into the castle with you.'

'But it's simple,' replied Friar Tuck with a little
chuckle. 'You see, she was hiding.'

'Hiding?'

'Yes, she didn't want to be seen. She was afraid
you might arrest her for stealing preserves from her
mother's pantry. And cakes. Silly little girl . . .' And

Friar Tuck patted Elvira's head indulgently.

The sentry looked puzzled.

'But *where* was she hiding?' he persisted.

'I can't stand people who keep asking questions,' thought Friar Tuck irritably. But aloud he replied, 'Behind *me,* of course. Like this.' And he walked in front of Elvira in such a way that she was completely hidden.

Despite his terror, Benedict wanted to laugh. The sight of Elvira cowering behind the friar's flowing robes made him feel as though they were playing some nonsensical game.

But the sentry saw nothing strange about this explanation. He smiled kindly at Elvira.

'There's no need to hide, my dear,' he said. 'We shan't put you in prison. Not if you're a good girl. You *will* be good from now on, won't you?'

'Y-yes,' replied Elvira nervously. And Friar Tuck, feeling that the conversation had gone on long enough, blessed the sentry again, took both children by the hand, and waddled through the gateway as fast as he could.

Not till they had crossed the drawbridge did he stop to wipe the sweat from his hot, red face.

'That was a near thing,' he muttered. 'He nearly had us. It's a good thing I've got a quick wit. Eh, children?'

'You were wonderful, sir,' agreed Elvira.

'Better than Robin Hood, eh? Don't you think so, my boy? Benedict, you're not listening.'

Benedict's eyes were fixed, indeed, on the two richly-dressed horsemen who had just come cantering into the castle courtyard. Friar Tuck looked down at the boy and saw that he was pale and trembling.

'What's the matter now?' he asked. 'Are you hungry?'

'T-t-those two men . . .' stammered Benedict, pointing to the splendid couple, who had passed through the gateway and were now approaching the heavy door that led to the spiral staircase.

'What about them? A bit overdressed, I thought. Not much taste.'

'One of them is Henry Shepherd.'

Friar Tuck turned to look at the two men, and his heavy jaw dropped.

'My God,' he gasped. 'The other one is the Sheriff of Nothingham. Come, we've no time to talk now.' And Friar Tuck hustled the children quickly along a meadow path which, he assured them, was a short cut to the main road leading to Sherwood.

But Benedict's legs were shaking so that he could scarcely walk.

'They must be going to my cell,' he moaned. 'They'll find me gone. They'll find the effigy. And they'll send out search parties . . .'

And even as he spoke, the alarm bell sounded from the castle watch-tower.

'Come,' muttered the friar, gripping the children's trembling hands. There's no need to be afraid. We'll get some farmer to hide us till the danger is past.'

But he did not feel quite as confident as he sounded. Already the fugitives could hear the cry of 'Escaped prisoner!' floating towards them from the castle keep, and the distant courtyard seemed to be full of running figures. The alarm bell continued to swing out over the watch-tower, and soon its urgent cry was taken up and echoed by every church tower in the surrounding countryside. Urgent and shrill, and drowning every other sound, the mingled bells came tumbling down the sky.

CHAPTER 12

London

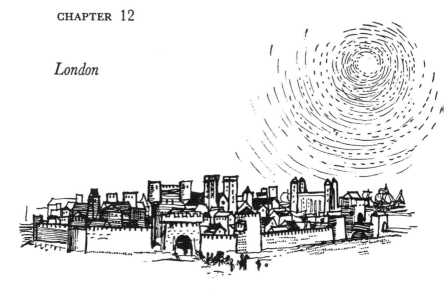

IT was quiet now in the dark fields, but Benedict was trembling. Though several hours had passed since the bells had warned Nottingham Castle of his escape, their harsh tongues still seemed to fill the night with terror.

'Hush,' murmured Friar Tuck soothingly as the children huddled for warmth into his heavy robes. 'As soon as the hunt has died down we'll get out of this stinking barn and make for Sherwood. I'm grateful to the good soul who has hidden us here, but it's not the most delightful of hiding-places.'

The hiding-place was, in fact, a decrepit barn filled with straw, rats and what smelt like rotting turnips. A kindly farmer had given the fugitives shelter there. It was only a tumbledown old barn, he assured Friar Tuck. He was thinking of pulling it down and building a new one in time for the winter. The Sheriff's men would not dream of seeking an escaped prisoner there. The smell alone would keep them away.

Though Friar Tuck did not share their host's

confidence, he accepted the shelter of the barn, and prayed hard. And sure enough, the Sheriff's men did not search there. The fugitives listened through a crack in the door as the good farmer told their pursuers how he had seen a priest and two children accepting a lift on a haycart bound for London.

And so they lay hidden in the barn till the hue and cry had passed. Then they thankfully said goodbye to their host and set out, along the moonlit tracks and dark alleys of the forest, towards Sherwood, where Sir Edward waited.

They reached Robin Hood's camp as dawn was breaking and stayed there hidden for several days, happy to be among friends again, until Tom, the lookout man, came one morning to tell them that the hunt was over. 'The Sheriff has called back his men,' he chuckled. 'He says he has better things to do than to send them scuttling all over the country in search of a petty horse-thief just to please Master Shepherd.'

Benedict did not particularly like hearing himself described as 'a petty horse-thief,' but he smiled when Tom added 'Henry Shepherd is as angry as a plucked hen. He still wants vengeance. But I think the Sheriff has lost patience with him.'

So now they were safe. And one bright morning, after a week of uneventful travel, they approached London at last.

'Once you see our great city you'll feel that all your troubles were worth while,' said Sir Edward happily, as he and the children set off after breakfast from the priory in Waltham Forest where they had spent the night.

Elvira bounced excitedly up and down in her pillion seat till Sir Edward complained that she was making him feel seasick. But Benedict did not care if the approaching city were London or Oxford or York. He was so happy to be free that he did not care about anything. They rode through the green arbours, bridle bells jingling, and the sun made the dewy leaves sparkle, and Benedict found himself singing the slightly ribald songs he had learned from the Outlaws. They were the only songs he knew. He had been brought up in a strict Jewish household, and did not know any of the popular songs that the troubadours took with them from inn to manor house, from village to great city.

As the forest began to open out, and paths and tracks converged into the broad road that led to London, the children gazed wide-eyed at the many different kinds of travellers who were bound – like them – for the capital. There were knights in dazzling surcoats, attended by gaily-dressed squires and pages; and merchants in richly furred robes, followed by pack-horses laden with merchandise; and priests and friars dressed in rough sackcloth, plodding painfully on foot or riding little grey donkeys; and huntsmen with falcons on their wrists; and men-at-arms with long, glinting lances; and archers with great bows slung over their shoulders; and tumblers and strolling players and troubadours with beribboned harps and lutes on their backs, and farmers carrying baskets of fruit and vegetables, hams and crates of squawking poultry. Sometimes an ox-drawn farm cart lumbered past. Sometimes a beggar trudged by, ragged and filthy and covered in sores, his palm outstretched, pleading for alms in a high, quavering voice. And once they saw, borne between two horses, a litter all draped in rich crimson cloth, and on the litter reclined a lady dressed in a fine blue kirtle edged with fur and stitched with gems, with a jewelled circlet on her brow and two long plaits of golden hair.

'Is that the Queen?' gasped Elvira, and Sir Edward

laughed as he replied 'No, poppet, the Queen is at Westminster. That is only a fine lady travelling from her manor to visit friends in London.'

'I wish I could ride like that,' said Elvira, feeling dissatisfied all of a sudden with her bumpy pillion seat behind Sir Edward.

'Perhaps you will one day.'

'We never saw anything like that in Lymford, did we Benedict?'

'London is *nothing* like Lymford,' Sir Edward assured her. 'Just wait till you *see* London. You won't be able to believe your eyes.'

And he was right. As they rode over the brow of Highgate Hill and the children caught their first glimpse of the City, its walls and turrets gleaming white against the blue morning sky, they could only sit silent on their horses, their eyes and mouths open in wonderment.

For London was a city all of towers and spires, its bells leaping from what sounded like a thousand steeples. The gates were crowned with beautifully ornamented turrets; the river, clear as crystal in the sunlight, glided past the walls like a great girdle of living silver, and all about the City were gardens and orchards and green meadows.

Sir Edward, excited as a schoolboy, pointed out the sights as they cantered through the meadows and the walls of the marvellous city rose up before them, white as newly-fallen snow.

'This is Moorfields,' he explained, as the horses picked their way over the damp grass. 'In winter it freezes over, and then the young lads skate on the ice or go sledging. I used to do it when I was a boy, and I'd do it still, if I wasn't too old.'

'How old *are* you?' asked Elvira curiously.

'Sssh!' said Benedict, scandalised, but Sir Edward

did not hear; he was calling out a cheerful greeting to the watchman at the gate-tower.

'They call this the Moor Gate,' he told the children as they cantered through the open gateway and found themselves, at long last, within the city they had not dared hope they would ever see.

'Welcome to London,' said the Crusader, suddenly grave, and the children looked about them with awe-filled eyes, as though it were Jerusalem.

It certainly was a fine city, its great stone houses surrounded by orchards and flower-filled gardens that sloped down to a river so clear that the children could see the fish twisting and gliding through the calm water.

'The Thames has more fish than any other river in the world,' boasted Sir Edward. 'Wait till supper, and you'll taste some of them. And did you ever see so many ships?' And he pointed out the many varied craft, their drifting sails richly coloured like jewels, as they lay at anchor off the cobbled quayside. Ships, he told them, from Bruges and Hamburg, Bordeaux and Rouen, Flanders and the Baltic and the sunny cities of Italy, their holds crowded with furs and lace and silks, salt and spices and rare wines.

The children gasped again as they reached Ludgate Circus and saw the huge cathedral church of St Paul's, half-built still, but magnificent even in its unfinished state. It would be over five hundred feet high, announced Sir Edward proudly, and the tallest church in all Europe. And then they passed through the Ludgate and out of the City again, and crossed the Fletebrigge and went cantering down Fleet Street towards the Strand, where Sir Edward lived, and where his wife, the Lady Matilda, was waiting to welcome him after his long journey.

At first the children were a little nervous as they

followed the knight into the great torchlit hall and Sir Edward's servants came to greet them. They had never before set foot in the house of a Christian nobleman, and the cavernous hall and all its rich yet sombre furnishings seemed strange to them. Then the Lady Matilda appeared; she looked very much like the lady in the horse-litter, with her beautiful blue kirtle, and the jewelled circlet on her brow, and her long golden hair. She curtseyed to her husband, and then came forward and kissed the children, and at the sight of her smiling face all their nervousness vanished.

At supper they tasted the Thames fish, as Sir Edward had promised – broiled crisp and brown and served up on silver platters, and followed by custard and candied fruit and pastry and French wine, and as they ate Sir Edward repeated the story of their adventures till the servants' eyes popped. Then a minstrel played sweet, mournful music on a harp, and the children began to feel pleasantly drowsy. In a kind of dream they felt themselves being lifted by two laughing serving-men and carried upstairs to the solar, where feather mattresses and soft fur coverlets awaited them. They were the most comfortable beds they had known in weeks, and they slept soundly till they were woken by the dawn clangour of the bells.

'We're going to Westminster today, to see the Queen,' announced Sir Edward calmly as they broke their fast that morning. Elvira was so taken aback that she dropped her bread honey side down on the rushes, and Benedict choked over his ale and had to be patted on the back.

'D-do you mean that *w-we're* going with you to see the Queen?' he stammered, as soon as he could speak. 'T-to give her the r-ransom money? Us?'

'Why not?' replied Sir Edward gravely. 'If it weren't for you, young sir, there would *be* no ransom money.'

'B-but I've got nothing nice to wear,' wailed Elvira, and Sir Edward roared with laughter.

It was the Lady Matilda who came to the rescue. In a very short time she had cut down one of her own kirtles for Elvira and found a page's suit that fitted Benedict. And that afternoon the three of them – Sir Edward looking magnificent once again in his Crusader's white surcoat and shining armour – went gliding up the river in a tapestry-hung boat, past green banks and swans and flowery verges, towards the Island of Westminster.

Many years later, when they were old, Benedict and Elvira were still to remember all the wonders of that day. They were to tell their grandchildren how the gates of the Palace of Westminster had opened for them; how richly-dressed guards had sprung to attention; how they had followed the Master of the King's Household through splendid halls and corridors to the small, tapestried chamber where Queen Eleanor awaited them. And how the Queen had thanked them, and smiled at the children as they knelt to kiss her hand.

As they left the Palace gardens and clambered back into the boat, the children could scarcely believe that their dangerous mission was over. The gallows at Nottingham Castle, the saddlebag crammed with gold, and Queen Eleanor's thanks, all lay behind them. 'Now we can begin to enjoy ourselves,' said Sir Edward with a smile as the Palace, and the great Abbey Church of St Peter where the Kings of England were crowned, melted into the leafy distance, and the crowded turrets of the City came to greet them across the shining river.

That afternoon he showed them more of the sights of London . . . the White Tower built by William the Conqueror, and the wonderful stone bridge being

erected across the Thames. They had been working on it for nearly twenty years, Sir Edward told the children, and it would have houses built on it from end to end, so that the people who lived there would be able to lean out of their windows and catch fish for their supper.

As the days passed the children came to know London and to share Sir Edward's love for that great city. They strolled along Cheap, with its rows of gaily-coloured booths, and explored the narrow, twisting back streets where jutting signs and overhanging gables almost shut out the sky and the cobblestones were thick with mud and slime. They visited the horse fair at Smithfield, and Benedict thought of the horse fair at Nottingham and shuddered pleasantly. They walked in the evenings past the fountains of Clerkenwell and Saint Clements, among the wise men and scholars who came there to discuss their books and enjoy the soft, summer air. They grew accustomed to the sounds of the city . . . the tick-tack of weavers' shuttles, the tapping of coppersmiths' hammers, the blacksmiths' ringing anvils, the thunder of hoofs on the cobbled streets, the market cries and the songs of people at work, and – rising above all other sounds – the joyful clamour of the bells. They saw brilliant processions . . . knights and noblemen, priests and choristers, and tradesmen in their gay Guild liveries. And once they even saw Prince John ride past with his retinue. He was fair and handsome, but the children did not like his expression, and they were glad that he was not going to be their king.

They also came to know Sir Edward and his wife better, and to feel at home in their great house. All the household, servants and pages, were soon their friends. Sir Edward's only son – his name was Robin and he was ten years old – was a page in the household of another knight, far away in Norwich, and his parents hardly ever saw him.

'No wonder she sometimes looks a little sad,' thought Elvira, watching the firelight flicker on the Lady Matilda's beautiful face as they sat at supper one evening. A tumbler was entertaining the company, and as he finished up with a final whoop and somersault their hostess looked a little wistful.

'Robin would have loved it,' she said.

'I daresay he sees plenty of jesters and tumblers in Sir Geoffrey's household, and maybe even better ones than this,' replied Sir Edward, but he did not smile.

'How terrible it must be to have your children brought up by other people. As strangers, almost,' said Benedict to himself. 'This would never happen among Jews. *We* believe in keeping the family together.' And then he felt a strange, sudden pang, and wondered if Elvira knew what he was thinking.

Next day he felt cheerful and lighthearted again. Sir Edward took the children for a ride in the country, and they explored the pretty villages of Stepney and Bethnal Green and stopped for a mug of ale at a farmhouse before cantering back towards London between hedgerows thickly threaded with wild roses.

They re-entered the City through the Cripple Gate, where the children had not been before. And as they did so, Benedict reined suddenly. Huddled in the shadow of the wall lay a cemetery, old and overgrown with the long grasses of Time, and his keen eyes had caught sight of the lettering on one of the fading tombstones. Weather-beaten though it might be, he recognised it as Hebrew.

'I'd forgotten you might want to see that,' said Sir Edward with a smile, as Benedict craned his neck to look closer. 'It's the old Jews' cemetery. Up till fifteen years ago all the Jews had to bring their dead here. Travelling hundreds of miles, too, most of them. An unpleasant journey, I should think. Then King Henry passed an edict permitting burial in their own cities. We'll stop for a few moments, if you'd like to look at the tombstones.'

Benedict nodded, and slid quickly from the saddle. It seemed very odd, here in London, in the middle of this wonderful adventure, to be reminded so unexpectedly of the past.

Hesitantly he walked among the slanting slabs of grey stone, picking out a name here, a date there, and Elvira followed, clutching at his hand and stumbling occasionally in the long, matted grass. The names had a familiar ring . . . Abram of Norwich . . . Vives of Cambridge . . . Amiot of Bury St Edmunds . . . Jews from all parts of England gathered together here in the shadow of London Wall . . . and Benedict felt a strange sadness rising in his throat.

Suddenly he stiffened and grew pale. His own name had sprung up at him from one of the tombstones. 'Benedict of Lymford,' the deeply-etched letters said. And underneath, in Hebrew, 'Baruch ben Shimon Halevi', and a date.

It was the date that reassured Benedict. 'July the fourteenth, 1173.' That was twenty years ago.

'Look, Elvira – we've found grandfather's grave,' he said, trying to keep his voice matter of fact, but aware that his legs were still trembling. 'My grandfather Benedict,' he added, turning to Sir Edward. 'He was a fine physician and scholar, Father told me. He could speak six languages. But he died quite young, when the plague came to Lymford.'

Benedict had often wished he could have known this learned grandfather whose name he had inherited. He had always seemed to the boy to be a figure in the dim past, almost as remote as Abraham and Moses. And now he had found him, here in the brilliant capital, with all its teeming life and colour.

All through the rest of the journey, Benedict was silent. Even when Sir Edward took them through Cheap and stopped at a booth to buy the children some sweetmeats, he said nothing. He did not see the jostling crowds, or hear their gay chatter or the traders' cries of 'What d'ye lack?' He was thinking hard. It seemed to him now that there had been no time to think since he and Elvira had arrived in London, more than a week ago.

'What are we doing here?' he said to himself. 'We belong in Oxford, with our own people. Not here, among strangers.'

And yet these people were not strangers any more, but his friends, and the house in the Strand was his home now. The more he thought about it, as they sat at supper that evening in the great firelit hall, the more he came to realise why he and Elvira had, day by day, been putting off the moment when they must journey to Oxford.

'We don't *know* Uncle Isaac and Aunt Ysabel,' he thought miserably, as he nibbled at a candied cherry. 'And they don't know *us*. They might not even *want* us to come and live with them.'

But despite these arguments, he knew what he had to do.

When supper was over, and the company began to drift towards the far end of the hall for a game of hoodman-blind before bedtime, Benedict plucked nervously at Sir Edward's sleeve, and the knight turned back and smiled.

'Sir,' said the boy, wishing hard that Sir Edward was not so kind. 'Elvira and I . . . that is . . . we feel we have taken advantage of your hospitality long enough. We should like to leave for Oxford tomorrow.'

Sir Edward looked taken aback.

'Has anyone offended you?' he said, after a pause.

'No, never, sir.'

'Then why do you want to leave us so soon?'

'Because we're Jews. And our home is in Oxford.'

Sir Edward sat down again on his great oak chair, and drew Elvira on to his knee.

'I *had* been meaning to speak to you children,' he said, 'and somehow I kept putting it off. But I suppose the time has come now.' He paused for a moment, and then added 'How would you like to stay here for good?'

'For *good?*' stammered Benedict, and Elvira gasped.

'Yes. How would you like to join my household?'

The children were too stunned to answer, and Sir Edward went on eagerly, 'My wife feels as I do. We're both lonely – with Robin away – and we've both grown fond of you. Playing your father so long, I suppose it's become a habit with me. Wouldn't you like to stay here, under my protection? There might even be a place for you at Court, Benedict, once King Richard learns how you served him. Life in London . . . you haven't seen half of it yet. There are pageants, and feasts, and tournaments, and river carnivals, and all kinds of marvellous things. And you would be safe here, safe for the rest of your lives. After all, do you know what awaits you in Oxford?'

Benedict had already thought of that, and his blood ran cold. Suppose . . . suppose Oxford should prove another Lymford? Suppose there should be a massacre, and no miracle this time to save him and Elvira?

Besides, he wanted very badly to stay in London. He loved Sir Edward and the Lady Matilda; he felt safe and protected in their house. The thought of the tournaments and the river carnivals and the splendour of the Court at Westminster tempted him enormously. In Oxford, life – if allowed to go on – would be monotonous and unexciting, just as it had been in Lymford. He would study all the time, and become a physician. Elvira would marry quite soon, and cook and spin and sew as a good Jewish housewife should. Very likely they would never see London again.

He glanced at Elvira, and wondered what *her* choice would be.

And then, all at once, the old cemetery at Cripple Gate, and one tombstone in particular, came into his mind. The dark Hebrew letters seemed to stare at him accusingly. Benedict of Lymford, dead now for twenty years, would never have believed that his grandson would one day consider abandoning his people.

With a sudden shock Benedict remembered that he and Elvira were the last survivors of the great scholar's family. If they chose to stay with Sir Edward their lineage would be wiped out. The older Benedict and all his kin would be truly dead at last. It would be as though they had never lived.

He had no choice. He knew that now.

'We . . . we *want* to stay here, sir,' he said. 'Really we do. But we can't run away from our people. Why else did we agree to go on this mission?' And here a sudden thought struck him. 'Besides,' he added, 'next week is my Barmitzvah, my confirmation. I *must* be home in time for that.'

Sir Edward slid Elvira off his knee, and stood up with a little sigh.

'I suppose I knew all the time what the answer would be,' he said. 'I shall miss you, but I understand. Early tomorrow morning you shall leave for Oxford.' He looked down at the children's solemn faces, and smiled.

'You had better ask the Lady Matilda to see that your saddlebags are packed,' he said. 'Then go straight to bed – you've an early start tomorrow. Rolf and Walter will ride with you, and we'll have no adventures *this* time. Off with you, now. I've a letter to write before I go to bed.'

After the children had gone, Sir Edward opened his coffer and took out a parchment roll, pen and ink. Then he spread the parchment on the coffer lid, sat down and began to write.

He addressed the letter to Sir Gilbert de Beaumont, Governor of Oxford, and went on: 'I am asking your protection, my dear friend, for the Jews of your city. I ask specially that you should watch over them, and come to their assistance with force of arms if ever they should be threatened by the mob ...'

CHAPTER 13

An Exile Comes Home

AND it actually happened that there were no massacres in Oxford, and the inhabitants of the Jewry lived there happily till King Edward I expelled all the Jews from England a century later. By that time the people in this story were dead, and it was their great-grandchildren who sailed across the Channel to a long exile in France. But all that belongs to history.

Three days after leaving London Benedict and Elvira reached Oxford, riding through the gates just as the sun was setting. They saw at once that it was a much bigger city than Lymford, though nothing, of course, like London. The streets were thronged with scholars on their way home from school, books and scrolls under their arms and ink-horns dangling at their girdles, and the bells chimed out peaceably over the darkening roof tops.

One of the schoolboys directed them to the Jewry, and as they cantered through the winding street with its massive stone houses, a sense of familiarity, of welcome almost, settled on the children. The street was empty, but as the horses' hoofs rang on the cobbles

135

first one face, and then another and another, appeared at the windows. Strangers were rarely seen in the Jewry, especially at this time of day.

The house of Isaac of Oxford stood on the corner of the Jewry, a fine house with glass windows and a heavy, brass-studded door. Benedict knocked a little nervously, and glanced back for reassurance at Rolf and Walter, the two manservants who had escorted him and Elvira to Oxford. They seemed solid and comforting . . . a last link, he felt, with Sir Edward.

'Suppose . . . suppose they don't want us?' whispered Elvira, clutching at Benedict's sleeve.

Benedict had thought of this many times. 'Sssh!' he whispered, as the heavy door swung open and a servant girl stood there, her eyes round with surprise and curiosity.

'I . . . I am Benedict of Lymford,' he said, trying to sound calm, and the girl drew in her breath sharply.

What happened afterwards was always to remain something of a jumble in the children's memory. A medley of new yet familiar faces, of greetings and embraces, of tears and laughter. In a kind of dream they met Uncle Isaac, a dignified figure in a rich furred gown; Aunt Ysabel, who looked almost like Mother, in her snowy coif and gold veil, though she was not quite so beautiful, and their cousins, Daniel and Janetta, who were just a little older than Benedict and Elvira. And when Uncle Isaac took them into his tapestried study, where a gold Menorah gleamed on a mother-of-pearl table, they felt as though they had never left Lymford. As though the past few weeks had been nothing but a piece of play-acting, or a story told by a troubadour.

'We heard what happened in Lymford, but we never dared to hope anyone was left alive,' said Aunt Ysabel, helping the children off with their dusty cloaks while Uncle Isaac seated Rolf and Walter on his best seats and poured wine for the travellers. 'Oh dear, I wonder if the soup is boiling over; I hope there'll be enough for everyone!' She seemed to be laughing and crying at the same time, and Daniel, who was standing behind her, caught Benedict's eye and winked. Benedict decided that he was going to like his new cousin.

As they sat down to supper, Uncle Isaac explained how he had come to know of the massacre. A merchant, passing through Lymford on his way to Oxford, had brought him the news. He had at once ridden to Lymford, but had found nothing but a burned-out, pillaged Jewry. The people he met had been unwilling to tell him anything, but one trades-man had invited him into his house and given him a cup of mead. Two men, he said, had been hanged because the fires they started in the Jewry had set light to some Christian houses; apart from that, no one had been punished. In the tradesman's solar Uncle Isaac noticed a pair of gold candlesticks that could only have come from a Jewish household.

'So that was that,' Uncle Isaac told the children, 'and I came home convinced that you were all dead. But, as you see, miracles still happen. Now tell me, what have you been doing these past weeks?'

So now it was Benedict's turn to speak, with Elvira interrupting whenever he paused for breath. Their relatives listened in fascinated silence, and Daniel's eyes opened so wide in admiration, and what even looked like envy, that it seemed they would pop out of his head. Only Rolf and Walter carried on eating and drinking stolidly. They had heard the story before.

There *was* enough soup for all of them, and it was followed by liver pasty and delicious roast goose. It was the first time Benedict and Elvira had tasted meat in weeks, and no one minded that they had double helpings.

The familiar flavour of the goose, cooked just a Mother had cooked it, and then the long Hebrew grace, chanted by Uncle Isaac in a deep, melodious voice, all helped to make Benedict feel thoroughly at home and at peace. He saw Elvira wistfully finger the embroidered velvet of Janetta's kirtle, and heard Aunt Ysabel promise to make her one exactly like it. And then he smiled to himself, and knew they had been right to leave London.

Early next morning Rolf and Walter set off home again, laden with gifts from Uncle Isaac. There was a silver goblet set with turquoises for Sir Edward, a roll of velvet for the Lady Matilda, and bales of cloth and sweetmeats for all the servants. Benedict did not feel sad any more as he stood at the city gates and watched them canter back along the road to London. They belonged to a part of his life that was over and done with.

But not entirely. He still had his own link with Sir Edward, though not even Elvira knew about it.

At the moment it lay in his coffer, in the loft where he slept with Daniel. A saddlebag containing a mysterious object so heavily wrapped in sheepskins and furs that it was impossible to guess at its shape, or the substance from which it was made. Sir Edward had tied it to his saddle just as he was about to leave for Oxford. 'A gift from me,' he had whispered. 'For your Barmitzvah, or whatever you call it. Promise you won't open it until that day.'

Benedict felt bound to keep that promise, but he could not help thinking about the hidden gift as his Barmitzvah came nearer.

By the time the day dawned, he and Elvira felt almost as though they had lived in Oxford all their lives. Their new family was their own family now. They knew all the inhabitants of the Jewry as if they had known them from babyhood. The days were peaceful and full of study; the evenings pleasant and harmonious as they sat round the supper table, sipping wine, and telling stories and parables, and singing Hebrew songs. And their great adventure grew more and more faint in their memory.

Though he had little time to prepare his reading from the Law, Benedict read it beautifully when the day came. In any case, the Jews of Oxford were all so impressed by his courage (for they had been told what had happened at Nottingham) that they would have admired him even if he had been struck dumb.

But he was not struck dumb. He made a speech later, at the feast which Uncle Isaac gave in his honour, and declared how happy he was to be back among his own people. And then Uncle Isaac made a speech, and so did all the leading citizens of the Jewry. And Elvira, wearing a new embroidered velvet kirtle that was even more magnificent than Janetta's, moved happily among the guests, offering them fruit and nuts and sweetmeats, and filling her own mouth when she thought nobody was looking.

It was nearly ten o'clock before the last of the guests took his leave. Benedict climbed wearily up the ladder to the loft, where his cousin was already asleep. The gables overhanging the window had a silvery glow.

Benedict looked up at the sky, so calm and spattered with stars, and thought how it also looked down on London, and on Sir Edward's house. The Crusader must be asleep long since, though the watchmen were wakeful in the gleaming towers overhanging the silent river. The time had come at last for him to open Sir Edward's gift, and he was afraid. He was afraid be-

cause there was only one thing he wanted the parcel
to contain, and he did not want to unwrap it and be
disappointed.

Slowly he went to the coffer, raised the lid, un-
fastened the saddlebag and lifted out the heavily
swaddled object.

'If it's not what I think it is, I shall die,' he
whispered to himself. 'It must be. It must . . .'

And then, with trembling fingers, he drew his knife
from its sheath and cut the rope that held the bundle
of skins together.

The outer fur wrapping dropped off, and with it
came a tiny parchment scroll addressed to Benedict.
He picked it up, his heart thumping violently, un-
folded it, and began to read.

'My dear Benedict,' Sir Edward had written. 'In
bestowing this gift on you I am restoring an exile to
its rightful home. I feel that those who owned it once,
and are now dead, would be glad to know that it is
safe in your care. I hope that it will be a source of
light to you and your children, just as it once
illuminated the darkness and proved a source of light
and understanding to me. And may you remember
what it did for both of us. Your true friend, Edward de
Bourg.'

Relief, and then joy, flooded through Benedict. He
knew now that his desperate wish had been granted.
There was not even any need for him to open the
parcel.

But he did open it, carefully removing layer after
layer of wrapping, till the shadowy loft suddenly
seemed to fill with golden light, and the thing that
had been in the parcel flashed between his hands,
jewelled branches curving upwards towards a great
six-pointed star.

It was the Menorah of Maxenburg.